T0171436

THE BOOK OF
POWER

Hugh D. Martin

iUniverse, Inc.
Bloomington

The Book of Power

Copyright © 2011 Hugh D. Martin

All rights reserved. No part of this book may be used or reproduced by any means, graphic, electronic, or mechanical, including photocopying, recording, taping or by any information storage retrieval system without the written permission of the publisher except in the case of brief quotations embodied in critical articles and reviews.

This is a work of fiction. All of the characters, names, incidents, organizations, and dialogue in this novel are either the products of the author's imagination or are used fictitiously.

iUniverse books may be ordered through booksellers or by contacting:

iUniverse
1663 Liberty Drive
Bloomington, IN 47403
www.iuniverse.com
1-800-Authors (1-800-288-4677)

Because of the dynamic nature of the Internet, any Web addresses or links contained in this book may have changed since publication and may no longer be valid. The views expressed in this work are solely those of the author and do not necessarily reflect the views of the publisher, and the publisher hereby disclaims any responsibility for them.

Any people depicted in stock imagery provided by Thinkstock are models, and such images are being used for illustrative purposes only.

Certain stock imagery © Thinkstock.

ISBN: 978-1-4502-9520-8 (pbk)
ISBN: 978-1-4502-9521-5 (ebk)

Printed in the United States of America

iUniverse rev. date: 1/24/2011

Acknowledgements

I would like to thank all the authors whose work has inspired me to write my own stories: Prof. John Ronald Reuel Tolkien, Prof. Clive Staples Lewis, Dr. Isaac Asimov, J.K. Rowling, David and Leigh Eddings, Eoin Colfer, and most especially Brian Jacques. And everyone who helped me when I got stuck and supported me in what started as a hobby but quickly grew to an obsession.

This, my first book is dedicated to my chief editor, who by absolute, total, 100% coincidence happens to be my aunt.

Notes from the Author

On the format of this book:

This story is divided into Episodes, a series of separate yet connected short stories. I based this format off of Saturday morning Japanese Anime cartoon shows like FullMetal Alchemist and Bleach. I chose this unique format partially because I thought it would be fun and partially out of the hope that this series will be *made into* a Saturday morning cartoon show.

On visual writing

The style of writing I use is based off of my all-time favorite author Brian Jacques, using vivid descriptions to paint pictures with the words. I also like to use those little screen gags you find in every cartoon show (I guess it would be text gags in this case). When I write I try to paint the picture of what you're reading in your mind. For example, in the fight scenes between Scott and Isaac I try to describe every blow and sword stroke they make to help the reader feel like a part of the action.

On Nature and how it fits in the story

The world this story takes place in is called Midaria, an Earth-like world that is in transition between the old world of magic and religion and the new world of science and technology. But where is it? William says it's 1525.14 light-years from Earth in direct conjunction with the constellation Orion, far on the outer rim of the galaxy. But is it really? It can be where ever you want it to be: another world in our galaxy, or one like Lewis's Narnia that can only be reached with magic, it could even be somewhere in this one. Perhaps Midaria is in our hearts and minds, in a place limited only by our imaginations.

I hope you enjoy reading my story as much as I enjoyed writing it.

Episode I
The Book

CHAPTER ONE:
A Day at the Fair

"Come on, guys, it'll be fun" said William as they drove down the road.

"Yeah, fun for you." retorted Jonathan Belmont, a blonde haired, blue-eyed teenager, who was currently driving the van, "I had plans for today but instead I'm stuck here driving us all to some stupid Renaissance Fair," he shouted.

"Calm down, Jon," said his twin sister Katherine, " let's just get there okay," she lowered her voice, "it's not like we have to *really* enjoy ourselves, it'll at least make William happy."

"Yeah, well why not make me happy" grumbled Jon.

"Come on," said William, "at the very least it'll be educational. We'll all have fun, right Scott?" he said, putting his hand on Scott's shoulder.

"Uh-oh," said Loki Burne, a lanky, brown haired young man, who had been watching from the back seat.

Scott Wolf was a tall, muscular youth who wore his long, brown hair in a ponytail over his left shoulder and had a single silver ring in his ear. He wore a green flannel shirt, blue jeans and hiking boots underneath a long tan overcoat, he also had on a pair of leather gloves with the finger tips cut off. He had been looking out the window since they'd started the trip, but at William's touch he seemed to wake up. He said nothing; he simply looked at William with his cold blue grey eyes. William looked at the older boy and shuddered involuntarily, he got the feeling that he should remove his hand or else and did so immediately.

Loki leaned forward in his seat, "Here's something to remember, Will," he said, "never, ever touch Scott."

"We're there," said Jon a little less than enthusiastically.

"All right," cried William, he would have jumped through the window had Scott not been sitting between him and the door.

Scott unbuckled his seat belt, slid open the door and stepped out. So this is a Renaissance Fair, Scott thought to himself as he looked at the virtual city of tents and trailers, not much to see, he thought. William was acting like a kid in a candy store, or maybe it was the sugar rush from all the soda he drank on the trip, Loki looked like he was enjoying himself as well.

"Okay everybody, gather 'round," said Jon, "we'll all meet back here at 3:00, okay."

"Fine by me," said William.

Scott looked at his watch. It was 10:30, and four and a half hours to look around and see the sights of the fair. With that, everyone went his or her separate ways, each to an event they wanted to see.

*　　*　　*

William and Katherine stayed together and went through the various events of the fair. They saw Jon and Loki at the Tournament grounds cheering like they were at a football game. William's raven-haired older sister, Isis stayed with them for a while, but then left to look for Scott.

"This place is kind of cool isn't it?" asked William.

"Yeah it is," answered Katherine, "you seem to know a lot about the Middle Ages."

"Not really," said William, "History isn't my best subject."

"Really," said Katherine, "you know, Scott knows a lot about History. Maybe you could ask him to tutor you."

"No thanks," said William, "I'll be fine on my own."

"Oh come on," said Katherine, "he's not *that* scary."

"Maybe not to you," responded William, "but you're not half his size."

That just made Katherine laugh.

*　　*　　*

Scott was walking past the various shops and stalls near the entrance to the fair. He figured he'd spend some of the $600 he made over the summer working as a camp counselor. As he passed by a red and white food pavilion, he saw a young boy at the counter trying to buy an ice cream cone, but the kid didn't have enough money. Scott reached into one of the pockets of his duster and pulled five dollars out of his wallet, he walked over and paid for the kid's ice cream, gave the boy the change. The little boy smiled, Scott smiled back. The boy ran over to his mother, "Mommy, mommy," he cried, "that nice man paid for my ice cream." Scott turned and walked away with a wry half-smile on his face.

*　　*　　*

William and Katherine had decided to sit down on a bench and wait for everyone else in their group. They saw Jon and Loki coming from the Tournament Grounds. "Wow", said Jon, "They had some cool sports in the Middle Ages".

"Yeah, I'll say", responded Loki, who was wearing a jousting tunic and drinking mead out of two goblets strapped to his helmet with a straw for each glass. William thought he looked funny. Someone pushed past him, it was one of the fair Jesters, and he didn't look too well. "What happened to you?" asked William.

"Some psycho hit me in the side of the head" the Jester replied.

On a sudden thought, Loki asked, "What did he look like?"

"He was tall with long hair in a ponytail, wearing an overcoat," said the Jester.

Loki, Jon and Katherine looked at each other, "Scott!"

"What did I do to your friend to get hit like that?" asked the jester.

"Who knows," replied Jon, "Scott's usually in a bad mood."

"Why?"

The friends didn't answer but they knew very well why. Eight years before Scott's mother had died in a car accident, an accident he had witnessed. He was so traumatized by the event that he spent the next three days crying his eyes out. William's big sister Isis had been the only person to give him comfort. He had even lived with William's family for a while until the court appointed a legal guardian, a public defense attorney named Roger Cromwell. Scott hated him, and said so frequently. Roger tried to get Scott to accept him as a father figure but to no success, the only person Scott had loved was his mother-and after his mother's death, Isis Evans-and sadly that wasn't ever going to change.

*   *   *

Scott was still looking for his souvenirs. He had passed by kiosks with jewelry and potions, useless and not his style. He came upon a place that looked interesting to him; it was YE OLDE BOOK SHOPPE. As he walked in, something immediately caught his eye, or rather someone. Isis Evans, Williams's older sister. Scott put his arms around her and kissed her cheek; his hand strayed to her behind and gave a firm squeeze.

"Scott, not here," she said pushing his hand away, "there are people around."

"I don't care how many people know how I feel about you," replied Scott.

They went outside, forgetting about the bookstore and kissed again.

"So" asked Isis, "what brings you here?"

"I decided to look for a souvenir, might as well get something out of this trip," responded Scott.

"Well, I don't think I'd look in there," said Isis, pointing to the bookstore.

"Ok," said Scott. "I'll see you later." He kissed her good bye and continued looking in other shops. He found one that looked promising and interesting, The Smithy. The shopkeeper was a big man with long, brown hair, blue grey eyes, a barrel chest and thick, brawny arms. He seemed familiar somehow, but Scott couldn't remember from where. The shopkeeper was at a large anvil banging on a red-hot sword blade. The glowing steel hissed as he dipped it in a tub of water to cool it, he asked, "What can I do for ye?" in a deep, gruff voice with a strange accent.

"Well I suppose I came here to buy a sword," Scott answered.

The blacksmith stroked his short trimmed beard thoughtfully, "Hmm, are ye left or right handed?" he asked.

"Right," replied Scott.

"Well then give this a swing", said the smithy, handing Scott a sword. It was a short sword, about a foot and a half in length and heavy for its small size. Scott swung the sword, with some difficulty.

"Hmm, a little too heavy," said Scott.

"Try this one," responded the smithy as he handed him a short saber, this one was not well balanced, when Scott swung this one it was hard to control.

"Not this one either," said Scott.

"Ah, well, I've just the blade for ye," said the blacksmith, as he moved to a dusty corner of the smithy. "I've had this for years, but no one's wanted it," he said as he pulled a long sword out of the pile. It was a Claymore-type blade, five feet long with long, straight crosstrees. Runic inscriptions went down the length of the fuller.

"Maybe I will", said Scott.

"Perhaps," said the smithy, "for 'tis a weapon fit for a king," he continued with a wink of his eye.

"How much?" asked Scott?

"500," replied the blacksmith.

Scott took out his wallet pulled out $500. "Here," he said. And that was that, Scott Wolf had bought a sword.

*   *   *

William had decided he wanted to buy a souvenir, so he dragged Katherine over to the shops. As they were walking, Scott stormed past them, carrying a sword in a scabbard, with a belt wrapped around the hilt.

"What was that about?" asked Katherine.

"I don't know," replied William.

They came up to YE OLDE BOOK SHOPPE. "Well," said William. "This looks interesting. Isis would like this shop, he thought as he walked inside. It was full of books on witchcraft and otherwise mystical subjects. Then he saw it; a huge book with a blue leather cover, runes were written on the cover. For some strange reason he did not yet understand, he felt himself gravitate towards the book.

"Welcome, children," came a soft, dusty sounding voice. The voice startled Katherine; she turned in the direction that it came. It was the shopkeeper, a small old man with a long blue robe, and half moon shaped glasses.

Katherine thought he looked like Professor Dumbledore from the Harry Potter books.

"Sorry I startled you, miss," said the shopkeeper, "I didn't mean too."

"That's okay," replied Katherine.

"So," said the shopkeeper quickly "What can I do for you? I have books on hexes, charms, spells and transfigurations."

"What's this one about?" asked William; pointing to the book he was walking towards.

"I don't know," replied the shopkeeper. "I've never been able to open it. For all I know it's a cookbook or something similarly useless."

"If it's useless to you, then I guess I'll buy it," said William, who was now looking forward to translating it. "How much do you want for it?"

The shopkeeper thought for a bit and then answered, "If you can open it you can have it."

"Okay," replied William, he stepped up to the book; it had an ornate, rotating metal lock worked into the cover. He stood there pondering for a moment, deciding how this complicated mechanism should work; on a sudden impulse he reached up and put his fingers into slots in the innermost ring. He turned it one-third the way around to the left then the lock clicked, a half turn to the right, *click*, then a quarter turn to the left, the lock popped open.

"Well I'll be Merlin's great-uncle Stefan," said the shopkeeper, "The book is yours, young man."

William picked up the book, which was very heavy. As soon as he and Katherine stepped out of the shop William's watch beeped. "3:00 already?" he groaned. "Come on Katherine let's go before Jon leaves without us."

When they got to the van, Jon was getting impatient. "I've been sitting here for an hour waiting for you two," he half shouted.

"That's because you came back at 2:00," said Loki from the back seat, "so shut up and drive."

Jon started the van and drove away from the fair, toward home.

*   *   *

The next day was Monday, a school day, but this fact didn't bother William in the slightest. Scott normally drove him and Isis to school, but today all three were driven to school in Roger's BMW 350i sedan. William and Isis sat in a very cramped back seat while Scott rode up front.

"Why did we have to take this thing?" complained Scott, who clearly didn't want to be there.

"Well, I'm sorry that this isn't that nice, roomy truck you've got," said Roger, rather sarcastically. "This is the only car I've got." Scott remained silent, while Roger continued. "You know, just once I wish you'd listen to me."

"Why?" asked Scott, "it's not like you care."

"Because," replied Roger, "I'm your father, Scott."

Suddenly the car screeched to a halt, Scott had pulled the hand brake.

"Let's get this straight Roger," Scott growled, "you are not now, nor have you ever been my father, and you never will be." Scott released the brake and the rest of the ride was spent in complete silence.

*   *   *

It was just another day at St. Andrew's High School; students packed the halls on their way to class. William always enjoyed his morning classes: English with the always-funny Ms. Mack, Physics with Mr. Thomas who was tough but fair, Math with Dr. Eppes who always had some funny demonstration on the importance of math in everyday life, and finally History with the school's favorite teacher: Mr. Hoke, his class was always fun, he played music during tests, showed a movie that went along with every lesson, and loved showing pictures of his travels to historical places around the world. Today's lesson was on the famous warrior and statesman: Caius Julius Caesar.

"Okay people," said Mr. Hoke, who, thanks to his habit of wearing tweed sport coats had earned the nickname "Professor Langdon" after the role played by Tom Hanks in the Da Vinci Code movie, "after conquering Gaul and marching toward Italy. Caesar said his most famous quote before crossing the Rubicon River, what were those words?" he was met with silence. He paced up and down the room; twirling the hockey puck with which he had won last year's championship for his team.

"Come on," he said, his face the picture of mock indignation, "we just watched a movie with this line yesterday. William?" he asked. William shook his head.

"Anyone?" asked Mr. Hoke, "Anyone? Bueller, Bueller." Some of the students giggled.

"Alea iacta est," said a deep voice from the far side of the classroom. Mr. Hoke spun around so fast that students thought he'd keep going and fall over; he stared incredulously at the student who heretofore had not said a word in class, Scott Wolf.

"Correct," said the teacher, just a touch unnerved.

✻   ✻   ✻

The lunch bell rang. Every student headed towards the cafeteria, gathering at the usual clique tables. The friends, William, Katherine, Isis, Scott, Jon and Loki all sat at their customary table at the back corner of the room.

"So William," said Katherine, "I've translated the symbols but not the words, it's written in a language similar to Gaelic. It's really weird. Maybe you can help me?"

"Yeah," said Loki, "Hey, Jon can't you speak Gaelic?"

"Some," replied Jon, "after all I am part Irish."

"Say this afternoon then?" asked William,

"Yeah, sure," came the reply.

"Ah great, here comes trouble," said Loki.

It was Chad, a tall, handsome student who considered himself quite the ladies man. He had tried to date every girl in the school, every girl that is except one: Isis Evans.

Chad sat down next to her and put on his best friendly smile,

"Hey Isis," he said, his voice soft and sweet, "you looking especially beautiful today."

"Get lost Chad," replied Isis, "you know that Scott doesn't like you."

Chad just shrugged nonchalantly,

"Scott doesn't have to know," he said, his smile widened showing his straight, professionally whitened teeth.

"I don't have to know what?" asked a growling voice from behind him and slightly over his head. It was Scott; he had walked up behind Chad as he flirted with Isis.

"Oh hey there buddy," said Chad disarmingly, "I didn't see you standing there."

Scott looked over Chad's shoulder at Isis,

"Is he bothering you?" he asked.

"Only a little," replied Isis, she stood up from the table and gave Scott a kiss on the lips.

"Come on," said Chad, "what does he do for you that I can't?" he asked Isis.

"This," said Scott simply, he gripped Chad by the shoulders and hoisted him up off the ground, then turned around and set him back down.

"Care for another demonstration," Scott said with a threatening crack of his knuckles. Chad could have outrun an Olympic sprinter as he headed frantically for the door. Scott calmly sat back down and lunch continued uneventfully.

* * *

On the ride home the only way you could have cut the tension between Scott and Roger, was with a chainsaw. For the most part the ride home was quieter than the ride to school. Scott and Roger just sat there, probably thinking of what to yell about, thought William. Fortunately, no one said anything the entire ride. They pulled up to Scott's house and Roger let them off.

"All right, you guys don't touch anything," he said, "Don't call me unless you absolutely have to, the judge doesn't like to interrupt court for phone calls." With that Roger drove away.

Scott shook his head. "Come on, he said, "let's go inside before we freeze."

It was cold out and William thought it might snow soon. Scott's house was like a kid's palace inside, with movies, video games and the ultimate sound system.

"Want some hot chocolate?" asked Scott.

"Are you kidding?" replied William ecstatically. Everyone knew that Scott made the best hot chocolate.

Scott walked into the kitchen, and got three mugs down from the cupboard, when there was a tapping sound on the window. Scott opened the window to see Loki standing there. "What, Loki?" asked Scott?

"Is Roger with you?" asked Loki.

"No," responded Scott.

"All right," said Loki. "I'm freezing out here."

A clicking sound came from the back door as Loki stepped in, holding a set of lock picks in his hand. "Hi guys," he exclaimed.

"Hi Loki," replied William as he continued playing one of the video games in the living room.

"What cha' makin'?" Loki asked Scott. "Hot chocolate! I want some." He added before Scott could answer.

Scott closed the window and got another mug from the cupboard.

"Here you go," said Scott, as he handed out mugs to everyone.

He made the hot chocolate with four large marshmallows, bits of peppermint, several kinds of chocolate and lots of whipped cream on top.

Loki and William continued to play video games while Scott and Isis snuggled on the couch. After being beaten by Loki 14 times in a row, William quit and Scott took over. Loki got smoked. When everyone was done playing video games, Loki made his rounds. He went straight to Roger's room, as he was looking around he saw something shiny and yellow – his favorite color- it was Roger's brand new Rolex watch. Loki picked it up and looked it over; it was one of the really nice ones with diamonds on the face. He pocketed the watch and continued to look around. By the time Loki was done looking around he had found: a set of gold cufflinks, a ruby stickpin and $14.50 in spare change. When Loki arrived back downstairs Scott was helping Isis with her coat.

"Bye Loki", said William.

"See ya," replied Loki.

Scott kissed Isis good-bye and she and William walked home.

"So," asked Scott, "what did you find?"

"A most excellent haul," said Loki cheerfully. "I cleaned Rodger's room of all that worthless junk," he continued.

"Hmm," was Scott's reply.

Scott and Loki continued their game until a pair of headlights shone through the window.

"Uh, oh", said Loki, "Roger's home."

Loki quickly packed up his stuff and ran to the back door as fast as he could. The back door was closed and locked just as Roger walked through the front door. All he saw was Scott sitting on the couch reading.

"Hello, Scott," said Roger trying to be friendly.

"Hello, Roger," said Scott not even bothering to look away from his book.

"Well my defense paid off, they dropped the charges," said Roger even though he knew that Scott was not listening.

"William Evans invited me over to his house," said Scott. "He wants to show me something."

"Are you sure it wasn't Isis?" asked Roger his voice practically dripping with a lascivious tone.

Roger was suddenly hit in the face and he fell to the floor. Scott had thrown the book at him. "Shut up," Scott growled. Scott stormed upstairs to his room, slammed the door and lay down on the bed.

∗ ∗ ∗

That evening, Mrs. Evans answered a knock at her front door. There stood a large young man, literally filling her doorway. It was Scott Wolf. "Hello, Mrs. Evans," he said with a very slight hint of cheer in his normally monotone growl of a voice. "Is William here?" he asked.

"Yes," replied Mrs. Evans with a bit of fright sounding in her voice. "William," she called, "One of your friends is here."

William half ran half trotted down the stairs. "Hi, Scott" he said, "Everything is downstairs." Both boys headed down to the basement. No one else was there so Scott took off his overcoat, sat down in a chair and fell asleep.

A short time later a van pulled up in the driveway with Jon and Katherine in it. Loki Burne pulled up in his blue sedan. The three were sent to the basement upon entering the house.

"Hi guys," said Scott rousing from his nap. He used the generic for everyone, since Katherine had been included in the "guys".

The three replied with a "Hi Scott."

William, who had gone upstairs, came back down with Isis. William had the book tucked under his arm. Isis sat down in the same chair as Scott. William sat on the couch near the table where he set the book.

"I've translated enough to at least know what the title says," explained William. "It's The Book of Power."

"Not much of a title," commented Jon.

William opened the book; the pages were covered in strange runes and symbols. He pointed to a line of runes and stated, "I've been working on deciphering this line here," he said pointing to a spot on the page. "I know what some of the letters are, but I have no idea as to what this word is, " he continued concentrating on the rune.

"Don't give yourself a headache," Jon chimed just before Scott silenced him with a slap to the back of his head.

William continued looking at the rune trying to figure out the language that it was written in. He did not understand and had no idea where to find out where it came from.

"Taisteal idir domhans" he said.

Suddenly the lights flickered and went out. The book started to glow, the runes transformed into shafts of white light. William became very scared. There was a flash of light and everyone blacked out.

CHAPTER TWO:
Ikaros

Scott's eyes snapped open; he quickly jumped to his feet; reached over his shoulder and drew his sword. Wait a minute, sword? Sure enough, there in his hand was the very blade he had bought at the fair. He hadn't brought it with him to William's house, so how did it get here? He then realized that he was no longer standing in William's basement, in fact he wasn't sure he was even in Michigan anymore. He was standing in a clearing in a forest. He looked down at himself--gone was his customary outfit. In its place were a tan colored wool tunic, brown trousers, weathered leather boots, and a dark green hood and cloak.

As Scott stood there wondering what exactly had happened to him, everyone else started coming around.

"What am I wearing?" said Katherine, finding herself in a long blue dress and petticoats, not an outfit she was accustomed to wearing.

"Katie?" asked Jon,"why am I dressed like John Wayne?" Instead of his usual polo shirt and slacks, he was wearing a night blue tunic, black pants, and a long black coat with steel pauldrons and vambraces. Combined with the black cowboy hat and blue bandanna, he did sort of look like he'd stepped out of a western movie.

"Did anyone get the license plate number of that bus?" asked Loki, he looked like he had a serious hangover, "What the hell happened to my clothes?" he asked when he noticed his outfit, a black tunic and trousers under an excessively pocketed leather vest.

"Where are we?" asked Isis, "and what am I wearing?"

She had found herself in a green dress which Scott thought brought out her eyes quite nicely, and a rather tight bodice, which accentuated her... assets.

"Hey, what happened to Will?" asked Loki.

William was sitting in the center of the clearing with the open book in his hands. He was wearing a ridiculous looking blue robe with celestial-themed gold embroidery.

"Will? Hey William?" shouted Loki, waving his hand in front of William's face.

"It's like he's frozen," said Katherine.

"I'll wake him up," said Jon, "Hey William, WAKE UP!" he shouted.

Nothing happened,

"Let me try," said Scott.

Everyone watched in shock as Scott lifted the sword above his head and brought it slashing down; in mid-swing he turned the blade so that the flat side hit William.

"Ow!" said William, "What did you hit me for?"

"It looked like you were in a trance." said Scott.

"Well you didn't have to hit me," retorted William.

"True," said Scott, "but it worked."

"Hey guys?" piped in Loki, "Where are we?"

*   *   *

"Where are we? How did we get here?" asked everyone.

"QUIET!" roared Scott, brandishing his sword.

"Now," he said, "let's figure this out, William where's that book?" It was the most William had ever heard him say.

"Right here," said William, showing the book to Scott.

"Find that passage you read," He ordered, "it might explain where we are." He turned to the rest of the group,

"All right," he said, "let's look around for signs of civilization," another uncharacteristically long-winded sentence. Everyone, except for William who was busy flipping through the book, started searching around the clearing.

"Hey, guys," called Jon, "I found something." Everyone, including William came running over.

"A road," exclaimed Isis, "let's follow it." So with Scott leading the way, everyone set off down the road.

*   *   *

William was having a dilemma. Although the book was now, quite strangely, written in English, he now noticed something he hadn't before. The book had over a thousand pages, and he had to find just one out of all of them. He flipped through it over and over, but he couldn't find it.

"Hey, guys," he said at last, "I found it." Everyone cheered William; he read the passage and found something rather troubling,

"Uh-oh," he said, "there's a warning label."

"What do mean a warning label?" asked Jon.

"Here's what it says," said William, "This spell is used to transfer a person or group from one world to another. However the caster can only use it once. For alternative spells see *Summoned Creatures-Abilities.*"

"Wait a minute," said Jon, "you can't use it again."

"That's what it says in the book," replied William.

"Find another one to send us back," said Jon his hand going to a sword on his belt.

William checked the back of the book for the relevant section, only to discover several dozen torn edges, the pages were gone.

"They're gone," said William, "the pages were torn out."

"What!" screamed Jon, "you can't find them!" he drew a rather interesting sword; it had an enlarged tip which gave it the appearance of a metal spear. Suddenly, a strong hand gripped his shoulder,

"I'd put that sword down if I were you," said a strangely accented voice. The voice belonged to a man in a gray overcoat who seemed to melt out of the foliage.

He was about the same height as Scott, with dark hair, and emerald green eyes streaked with silver. His rugged, unshaven features made him look perfectly suited to the environment.

"Put the sword down now youngin'" said the stranger. Scott leveled his sword at the stranger.

"Who are you" he growled.

The stranger took his hand off Jon's shoulder and gave an elegant, flourishing bow,

"My name is David," he said, "I am simply a Wanderer down the paths of the world."

"And what do you want?" asked Loki, putting his hand on a dirk at his belt.

"I don't want anythin'," replied David, "I heard your shouting and thought you were in trouble, so I came over to investigate…" his voice trailed off when he saw the book William was carrying.

"Where did you get that?" he asked with a bewildered expression on his face.

"What, this?" asked William, holding up the book, "I bought it at a fair." David gave that a rather strange expression.

"It's how we got here," said Jon.

"What?" said David. "How did that happen?"

They explained their situation to the stranger. He absorbed it all in silence, but finally opened his mouth to say, "Holy wah," and fainted.

"What was that about?" asked Loki, Scott just shrugged his shoulders. The group started down the road again

"We can't just leave him here" said Isis. Nobody moved

"Well, don't everybody get up at once" said Scott, and with a grunt he picked up the unconscious David, threw him over his shoulders.

*   *   *

They had gone a little way further and the road had improved somewhat before they spotted a signpost.

"Ikaros, 5 miles" read William.

"Sounds like a town" said Loki.

"Good," said Jon, "someplace we can ditch woods boy over there." He flicked his thumb over his shoulder at the unconscious David.

"I hope there's a hotel or something," complained Loki, "my feet are hurting for all this walking."

"Shut up, Loki," said Jon, "a little exercise is good for you."

The path took them out of the forest into a cluster of hills. When they came to the top of the highest hill they saw a small, medieval town, it looked like it was taken right out of a history book. There were high, crenellated walls all around and an impregnable looking castle in the center of town.

"Well," said Loki, "I guess I was right about it being a town." The six of them started down the hill towards the main gate.

Scott shifted his burden with a grunt, "this guy's heavier than he looks" he said.

"Well then," said Jon helpfully, "why not share the load."

"Okay," replied Scott, letting David's weight slip off his shoulders, right on top of Jon. David's mass, times his acceleration off Scott's shoulders equaled a sufficient amount of force to propel Jon into the dirt.

"That's not what I meant," said Jon.

"I know," Scott replied with a smile.

"Hey, give that back" shouted William. Someone in a black hood and cloak had crept up on the group and grabbed the book from William's hands and ran towards the castle.

CHAPTER THREE:
Changes and Plans

It was at this moment that Scott did something that even he wasn't quite sure about. Quick as a flash, he reached up behind him and in one smooth, almost choreographed motion drew his sword and threw it. The enormous blade barely missed the thief's head and thudded point first into the dirt. The thief stopped and looked back. William saw that he was a young man with intelligent, blue grey eyes, an unruly tuft of white hair stood out above his brow. That was all he saw before the book-thief turned and ran. Scott took off after the bandit, pulling his sword out of the ground as he passed.

"Well," said Jon, "better go get him before he kills someone." His voice was surprisingly calm.

"Yeah," said William, "and we can get my book from him too."

"I wasn't talking about the thief," said Jon. They started to follow Scott.

"Hey!" shouted Katherine, "We can't leave David here" she said, Jon groaned. Everyone went and helped carry the unconscious Wanderer. Scott was right, he was surprisingly heavy.

*   *   *

Scott pursued the book-thief through the town. The black-cloaked figure led him towards the castle. Scott quickened his pace, he could tell the thief would soon tire out, and when that happened that black cloak would turn red. The bandit suddenly put on a burst of speed as he neared the castle. No sooner had the cloak passed over the drawbridge than two guards in red robes and chain-mail sprang from behind the gate and grabbed the thief.

"Hey," called Scott, "that's mine." One of the guards looked at him and said something he couldn't make out. Scott raised his sword and charged forward. The other guard raised his hand and muttered something. Scott felt like he'd been hit in the gut and literally flew backwards, his cloak billowing around him.

* * *

The rest of the group struggled to carry David through a somewhat crowded courtyard across from the castle, when a large, green blur shot in front of them and crashed into a low stone wall that surrounded a garden.

"What was that?" asked Jon, dropping David's feet and heading over to investigate. He found a very angry Scott Wolf sitting in a small pile of rubble and ruined flowers.

"What happened?" asked Loki, Scott's only answer was a snarl.

"Hey! You!" came a voice; it was the home owner, "What're yew doin' crashin' into my house?" Scott's fury found a new target; he walked towards the small man with a growl.

"Yew do anythin' ter me an' I'll have the town guards on ye" said the home owner. Scott snarled angrily and swung his fist. The force of the blow was sufficient to crack the frame of the front door. The man in front of Scott stared for a moment, then fainted dead away. Scott sheathed his sword, hoisted David on his shoulders and walked away.

* * *

"Rooms for all of ye?" said the disbelieving innkeeper. Never before had he had so many patrons at once.

"Yes," replied William, "we had quite a trip today."

"Any trouble with 'ighway men?" asked the innkeeper.

They shook their heads.

"Alright," he said, "that'll be sixty-four gold pieces." Here the group had a problem; none of them had any money. Scott, fortunately, found a solution, checking David's coat pocket. He pulled out a jingling leather bag; he counted the required amount out of it, gave the coins to the innkeeper and put the bag back in David's pocket.

"Right this way" said the innkeeper with a wave of his hands. He led them down the hall and up stairs to a small, comfortably furnished common room surrounded by eight bedrooms.

"Adequate," pronounced Scott gruffly. They laid David on the bed in one of the rooms and sat down at the common room table.

"Well," said Katherine, "we might as well make ourselves at home."

Loki plopped into an armchair, "Man, I'm bushed." Isis and Katherine sat down in the other chairs while Jon stretched out on a couch.

"What are we going to do?" said William, "who knows what that thief will do with that book."

"I'm not so sure he has it any more," said Scott.

"Why?" asked William.

"The castle guards took it," answered Scott.

"What's in the book?" asked Katherine.

William scratched his head, "well," he said, "there are spells in it that are for controlling gravity, probability, and I few that I think violate the known laws of physics."

"Sounds like if you have that book, you can do what ever you want," said Jon.

"Exactly," replied William.

"Hmm, that could be useful," said Loki with a waggle of his eyebrows.

Jon gave Loki a disgusted look, "Loki," he said, "I know what you're thinking, and that's just wrong man."

"Hey," said Loki with a smile, "a guy can dream can't he."

"What about David?" asked Isis "is he going to be all right?"

"He'll be all right," said Scott, "all he needs is rest."

"Well," said Jon, "I think we're about done here." He got up off the couch and went down stairs.

*   *   *

Scott and Loki followed him downstairs to the taproom. Jon ordered three pint tankards and brought them to a table.

"Sit down," invited Jon, "this'll take your mind off the fact that we're trapped on another world, who knows how far from home, and have no way or hope of getting home within our lifetimes."

"That was quite a mouthful," said Loki, who was giving the inside of his cup a strange look.

"Well," said Jon, "do you have a shorter way of saying it?"

Loki looked around the room,

"Yes," he said, "but nothing I can say in polite company."

Jon chuckled. "I figured as much" he said.

Loki took a sip and made a face, "What is this anyway?" he asked.

"Ale," said Scott.

"Uugh," said Loki with a disgusted look on his face, "I can't drink this." He went up to the bar and came back with three pints of a golden yellow liquid.

"What's that?" asked Jon.

"Mead," declared Loki proudly, "the chosen beverage of ancient kings".

Jon took a sip of proffered beverage, "Sweet," he said, "What exactly is it?" "Fermented honey," answered Scott, "I'm not sure exactly how they brew it."

"I don't care how they make it," said Jon, "just bring more!" He happily chugged the tankard.

Loki looked across the table at Scott. "So what happened at the castle?" he asked.

Scott slammed his cup down on the table. "I missed," he said.

"How's that a problem?" asked Jon.

Scott grabbed a knife off the table and threw it at the dart board on the far wall; it stuck an inch deep dead center.

"Oh yeah," said Jon sheepishly, "I forgot about that". For the past three years at the summer camp he worked at, Scott had been hatchet-throwing champion. His throwing skills also carried over to knives, darts, and books to Roger's face.

"Okay so you missed a throw," said Loki. "That happens, but what happened when you got to the castle?"

"I don't really know," Scott confessed, "one of the guards said something and next thing I know I'm flying into a bed of hydrangeas."

That was all that Loki could get Scott to say about what had transpired. So the three enjoyed their drinks, Scott nursing a single tankard, Loki taking healthy sips, and Jon gradually chugging his way towards cirrhosis. Finally, Scott pushed his still half filled cup away, Loki had a fine buzz, and Jon collapsed face first onto the table. Loki paid the tab while Scott picked up Jon and they went upstairs to bed.

*　　*　　*

Early the next morning, Loki woke up to the quiet. The only sound was the clock on the wall. He got out of bed and walked into the common room and found Scott Wolf sitting in an armchair, reading.

"Um… good morning Scott," said Loki a little startled. Scott merely grunted and continued reading. Loki sat down and had a pleasant conversation with Scott, well as much of a conversation you can have when your companion doesn't talk. Suddenly they heard someone screaming. It came from one of the rooms around them. In a flash Scott was on his feet, sword drawn and Loki ran to the door, dirk in hand, and kicked it open. Katherine was sitting bolt upright in bed, her eyes wide with fright.

"What happened?" asked Loki.

"Hmmph," said Scott, "bad dream," he sheathed his sword and went back to his book.

"That was weird," said Katherine.

"What happened?" asked a very sleepy looking Isis and William, "was somebody screaming?"

"Kat had a weird dream," Loki told them.

"What did you see?" asked Isis.

Katherine concentrated to remember.

"I was standing in a large room inside that castle," she said, "There was this man in a black cloak standing there. I couldn't see his face but he had these sad grey eyes. Then I saw Scott standing in the same spot holding his sword. He had his hand over one eye and was bleeding like he was in a fight and he fainted."

"A cardinal rule I live by," said Loki, "when Scott faints, you're in deep trouble."

Everyone felt a little worried about that. Fortunately William had an idea to change everybody's mood.

"How about we go downstairs and have breakfast," he suggested.

"Good idea Will," said Loki, "I think we could all use some decent food after all we've been through."

Everybody headed for the stairs, but Scott stayed in his chair.

"Come on Scott," said Loki, "breakfast is the most important meal of the day."

"I already ate," said Scott not looking up from his book.

"Okay," said Loki, "suit yourself." He headed downstairs with the rest of the group. Scott was left by himself, a man in a black cloak, he thought, could be the thief I was chasing yesterday. He was interrupted by a loud groan coming from behind one of the doors; it opened to reveal an extremely hung-over Jon Belmont.

"Did anybody get the license plate of the bus that ran over my head?" he asked.

"You could check in the empty barrel behind the bar downstairs," said Scott matter-of-factly.

"Where is everybody?" asked Jon.

"Downstairs having breakfast," answered Scott.

"Not you," said Jon.

"Already ate," replied Scott.

"Okay," said Jon, he half walked-half fell down the stairs to the dining room. Finally, thought Scott, peace, quiet, and a good book.

* * *

Downstairs, everyone was enjoying a healthy, delicious breakfast of pancakes, eggs, and thick sliced bacon.

"Morning," called Jon.

"Hey Jon," said Loki, "pull up a chair and have some breakfast. The cook here's just as good as Scott." It was a term of high praise among the friends. Jon got a plate and helped himself to the buffet table.

"So how come Scott didn't join us?" asked William.

"He's an early riser," said Jon, "he's usually up and about before sunrise."

"Ah," said William, "a student of Benjamin Franklin". Jon gave him a quizzical look.

"Come on," said William, "you know." He and Loki said as one,

"Early to bed, early to rise, makes a man healthy, wealthy, and wise."

"Hear, Hear" said several other tavern patrons, raising their coffee cups.

"Hmm," said Katherine, "guess it applies on this world too."

"You know," said Isis thoughtfully, "I'll bet Scott is still hungry". She filled up a small plate and took it up to the common room.

"Why'd she think that?" William wondered aloud.

"Ever seen Scott eat?" asked Katherine.

"No," said William.

"William," said Loki, "Scott could probably eat your body weight in breakfast."

"Wow," said William.

The four friends sat chatting over their meal for a while then headed back upstairs too find Scott and Isis chatting amiably over a short stack. Oh sure, thought Loki, he talks to her. They all sat in silence until Jon said what was on everyone's mind,

"So, how are we going to get the Book back?"

"Give me a set of lock picks and a diversion and I'll have us in there quick as a flash" he snapped his fingers to emphasize his point. Then something rather strange happened, from Loki's perspective everything froze: his friends in the common room, the people still eating downstairs, even the bird flitting by the window. Loki was very much freaked out; he also had a sharp pain developing between his eyeballs. It was kind of eerie seeing everything just hanging there. On a sudden instinct he snapped his fingers again.

"What's wrong Loki?" asked Katherine seeing his bewildered expression.

"You were all frozen," he said.

"What?" said Jon incredulously.

"When I snapped my fingers, everything froze like…" his voice trailed off.

"Like what?" asked William.

"You guys will probably think I'm going nuts, but, it was like time just stopped."

"Stranger things have happened," said William.

"Yeah," said Jon, "just look what happened to us."

"Can we get back on topic," growled Scott, "William, you were in AP Physics right?"

"Yeah, why?" answered William

"Well," said Scott, "try to think of something to knock down the door."

"Oh sure, do it the hard way;" said a voice, it was David.

The assembled friends were relieved that he had recovered.

"How long were you listening?" asked Loki.

The Wanderer smiled. "I woke up at 'Can we get back on topic,'" he replied in a flawless impression of Scott.

"What did you mean by 'the hard way'?" asked William.

David sat down in an armchair and scratched his chin thoughtfully.

"As I recall, there are some secret passages that lead under the castle" he said.

"That's good," said Katherine with a sigh of relief, "we can just sneak into the castle, grab the book and then get back out."

"Then hopefully get back home," said Jon, "assuming of course we know where we are to begin with."

"You're on the island of Ikaros, on the world of Midaria" said David.

"Alright, we know where we are," said Scott, "now, how are we going to get inside the castle?"

David sat back thinking for a bit,

"Okay," he said, "here's the plan…"

CHAPTER FOUR:
Nightfall at the Castle

Under cover of darkness, seven shadows made their way through the city streets towards the castle. Mikan, a low ranking castle guard patrolled the outside of the moat when he heard a strange cracking sound. He looked and saw the man on the other patrol drop to the ground with his head cocked at a funny angle. Mikan held his spear point out in front of him as he crept over to investigate.

"Don't move," said a voice, a slim blade held against his throat. Mikan was a rather big man, and he easily threw his opponent to the ground. His attacker was a lanky young man in black clothing, a thief. Mikan was about to apprehend the trespasser when a large hand with a big sword crashed down on his helmet. Mikan dropped like a stone, unconscious.

"Next time just get it over with," growled Scott.

"Sorry," said Loki, "he caught me by surprise."

Scott grabbed his friend by the front of his shirt and hauled him up,

"That's no excuse," he said.

"Hey, over here," called David in a whispered version of a shout. He was brushing dust off the wall with his hand,

"Here it is," he said. He pushed his finger into a small crack, and with a muffled grinding sound, the door opened.

*   *   *

"Come on, this way," said David as led the way down the passage.

"How much farther?" asked Katherine, as she wasn't all that fond of dark places.

"We're almost there," said David calmly as they approached a tunnel that seemed to stretch off into the blackness.

"Down that way?" asked Loki, he was a little nervous as well.

"Hmmph," said Scott and he walked down the tunnel with only the soft stumping of his boots to reveal his presence. David took a torch from somewhere under his coat and lit it,

"Come on," he said, "there's nothing to be afraid of". They followed him down the passage until they came upon Scott pounding his fists on the wall before him. "This is the way out," he said. David reached for the switch on the wall.

"Already tried," said Scott, "It's jammed."

"What if we all tried pushing it?" suggested William.

"That might work," said David. Everyone braced against the wall and pushed with all their might but the door only moved a crack.

"This is gonna take all night" said Jon.

"You got a better idea?" asked Loki with scarcely concealed sarcasm.

"How about trying that switch again," retorted Jon.

"I just said it's jammed," growled Scott, "now keep pushing, if we get it open far enough it should open all by itself."

They pushed as hard as they could again and sure enough, the door mechanism caught and opened automatically, revealing a very well furnished hallway on the ground floor of the castle.

"Told you," said Scott with a wry half-smile.

"Hey you! Stop right there!" came a shout, and two heavily armed guards came running down the hall. Scott and Jon drew their swords.

"Leave us alone!" commanded Isis; the guards were suddenly thrown backwards into a wall by some unseen force.

"Whoa," said Loki, "what was that?"

"I don't know," said Isis, "I think it was me."

"What ever it was, it sure was helpful," said William.

"Let's get a move on," said David snuffing out the torch, "this way". Suddenly a charge like electricity surged through the air around them.

"What was that?" asked Katherine.

"I hope that wasn't what I think it was," said David nervously. He started running towards the central tower of the keep; the group followed him, those with weapons held at the ready. Another charge surged through the air; David swore loudly and went up the stairs as fast as he could.

*   *   *

Meanwhile, another group was also trying to infiltrate the castle, though their goals were far more dubious. The three thieves were tunneling under the walls, and planned to come up in the courtyard.

"Oh come on, you guys," said one of them, a nervous young man with dark hair and bright, hazel eyes, "it's foolproof, we tunnel into the courtyard, break into the castle and help ourselves. What's so hard about that?"

"I just think we're rushing into this, James," said the young woman with fiery, red hair and emerald eyes.

"Yeah," agreed the small, cat-like man with iron gray hair who was digging for all three of them, "Jessia's right. A hasty thief is a captured thief."

"Shut up, Krant," said James and cuffed the older man on the back of the head.

"Ow," said Krant and tried to retaliate but James pulled his dagger. The three kept digging until they broke the surface in the courtyard. James and Krant crawled out first, to find a tall young man in a black cloak making his way across the space. He was quite surprised to see them,

"Oh, hello," he said politely, "trying to get into the castle?" His voice had a refined, cultured accent.

James sat back and blinked in surprise, Krant pulled a small knife from one of the many pockets on his leather vest,

"Who wants to know?" he demanded.

"Just a man who's lost something important and is trying to get it back" said the black-cloaked youth.

"Well, then," said James, "I suppose, we could work together."

"What's this," said Jessia in mild disbelief, "James, deviating from the plan, the world must be coming to an end."

The cloaked youth chuckled softly, it seemed like he was unused to the sound,

"That's alright," he said, "I don't need to put you in danger." He walked up to a wall, flung up a grabbling hook, and climbed into a window.

"That was strange," said Krant. The thieves crept up to a door and found it locked,

"Time for the master to go to work," said Krant. He pulled a thin, needle-like implement from a pouch on his belt. He slipped the pick into the keyhole and three seconds later, opened the door. The raggedy little man smiled to himself, put away his lock pick, and began searching for valuables. Jessia and James followed him in.

"Come on," said Jessia, "let's check upstairs." They exited the room and came across an ornate mahogany staircase.

"Keep to the edges," cautioned Krant, "A creaky stair is the end of even the best thief."

"Right," said James. He walked up the stairs and a loud creak sounded. Krant slapped his forehead while Jessia drew her sword to repel any guards. No one came.

"Whew," said James with a sigh of relief. Krant thwacked him on the back of the head.

"Next time listen to what you're told," the older man berated them.

"Ow," complained James, rubbing the sore spot on his head. The three comrades went up the stairs and found a pair of guards slumped on the carpet.

"Are they dead?" asked James.

"No," said Krant, "just knocked out for a while." He pointed to a sizeable dent on one of the guards helmets.

"What happened?" asked Jessia.

"Probably that guy we met in the courtyard," said James.

"There's nothing here," said Krant, "so let's move on." They headed down the hall to a room near the central tower.

"Jackpot!" declared Krant when he went inside. The room was filled nearly to bursting with gold: coins, plates, goblets and jewelry. There was gold in every conceivable form. James frantically stuffed the loot into some bags he had brought. Jessia tried on jewelry in front of a full length mirror. Krant however kept looking for more things to steal.

"Hey," said Jessia, as James grabbed a ruby studded necklace from her hand and unceremoniously threw it in a bag.

"Hey you two," called Krant, "over here." Jessia and James dragged the bags of gold down the hall to where Krant was in the dining room.

Laid out on the table was a meal fit for a dozen kings. A grilled haunch of an elk lay on a platter in the center, surrounded by roasted quail and garnished with sage and parsley. Goblets of fine wine were placed at each setting next to fine china plates and tableware cast from the finest silver.

"Let's eat," said Krant. The trio of thieves sat down and helped themselves to sumptuous meal.

*   *   *

David led the way up the stairs.

"Come on," he said, "We have to get to the top." He sounded desperate.

When they reached the top of the stairs they felt another charge from a bolt of chain lightning. Everyone but Scott cringed as the bolt shot by them.

"Come on," said David, still wincing from the shock. They hurried to the door.

"It's locked," said Jon.

"Allow me," said Loki, reaching for his lock picks.

Scott drew back his boot and kicked the door off its hinges. The force of the impact was sufficient to cause the door to splinter. What was left of the door crashed to the stone floor

"Let's go," said David, leading the group through the doorway.

＊　　＊　　＊

Crash. The table shook, making the plates rattle.

"What was that?" said Jessia.

"Sounded like a cannon going off," said James.

"They don't have cannons on this island, remember," said Krant not bothering to look up from his meal.

The three thieves continued eating their meal.

＊　　＊　　＊

The doorway led down a narrow hallway into a broad, circular chamber. In the center of the room was a small altar. Set upon it was the open book. Standing reverently before the book was a dark, sorcerous figure with a silver crown on his head, the king of the castle. He was tall and thin with long white hair and a beard with touches of black at his ears and chin.

The old sovereign was so absorbed in the book that he was oblivious to Scott silently approaching from behind him with drawn sword. Scott raised the blade above his head with both hands and brought it down in a swift chop. The strike never landed as a translucent bubble of energy sprang into being around the king and Scott's sword bounced off.

As Scott stood there with a bewildered expression on his face, David addressed the aged monarch.

"That book doesn't belong to you."

The king turned to see who had spoken to him. He was clearly surprised to find other people in the room and responded in a deep, basso voice.

"Who are you?"

"I'm the man who's going to keep that book out of the wrong hands," said David. The Wanderer pulled a large handgun out of his coat that didn't look like it belonged in the medieval setting of this world.

"This book is ultimate power," said the king, covering it with his hands, "I will not allow you to take it from me!"

He threw his hand forward and lightning flew from his finger tips. The spell was aimed at David, but diverted towards Scott, or rather Scott's sword. The magic was absorbed by the blade and sword started to glow.

"What!" said the startled king, who hurled lightning again, this time at Scott. The same thing happened and the sword glowed brighter. Jon leaped forward, sword at the ready. The king crossed his arms in front of himself, another bubble of energy forming around him and Jon's sword bounced off harmlessly.

"That's not fair," said Isis. She pointed her finger at the king, and out of nowhere a bolt of lightning sprang from her hand and struck him.

"What was that?" asked Jon.

"I...don't know," said Isis.

Taking advantage of the confusion, Scott made his attack. The king raised his arms in defense again; Scott's sword absorbed the shield and struck the mad monarch. There was a tremendous shockwave and the king flew back against the wall.

A man came in through another door during the fight. He was not very tall, with a wiry frame and narrow, rodent like features, "Your Majesty!" he cried.

Jon walked up to the man and pointed his sword at his chest.

"Who are you," he demanded.

The man stepped back, smoothed the creases of his midnight blue robes and said in a reedy voice.

"My name is Malagent; I am His Majesty's Chief Advisor and Royal Justiciary."

Jon cocked his head curiously,

"Royal what," he said, obviously never having heard the term before.

"It means Royal Police Chief youngin'," said David. Jon nodded at the explanation and continued to threaten Malagent.

"You will release me at once," declared Malagent, "perhaps I might be lenient at your trial."

"Trial!" shrieked Katherine.

"You did kill the king," said Malagent, "and for that you are to be placed under arrest." He snapped his fingers and several guards entered the room, weapons drawn. They took positions around Malagent and pointed their swords at the group. Jon suddenly found himself facing a dozen sharp points. He gave a weak chuckle and backed down.

"Now what?" asked Loki.

"Now we fight," growled Scott. He stepped to the fore and held his sword ready. The guards spread out and prepared for battle.

"You're going to regret that choice," said Malagent. He snapped his fingers once again and the guards charged forward, then stopped. It was almost as if they had become frozen in place. The guards looked around confused. Only William noticed that David was holding his hand slightly in front of him, palm open.

"What's happening?" asked Katherine.

"Sorcery!" cried Malagent, "Kill them! Now!"

"Sorry, not going to happen," said David. He threw his hand forward as if pushing something away. The guards and Malagent flew back into the wall.

"Run for it youngin's!" shouted David. They were only too happy to oblige. William grabbed the book and ran as fast as he could down the stairs. Once they reached the bottom Loki turned to head back toward the secret passage.

"Forget it, youngin'," said David, "the guards will have sent a patrol down there by now."

They headed down the hall in the opposite direction. Eventually they came to the main hall just inside the door, but they weren't the only ones there. A large group of guards had been lying in wait for them, but they were all scattered around the floor knocked unconscious, there was a tall figure in a black cloak standing in the middle of the room.

"You," growled Scott, recognizing the book-thief.

The young man raised an eyebrow quizzically,

"Do I know you?" he asked.

"You're the guy who stole my book," said William, also recognizing him.

"Your book?" said the thief cocking his head, "I could have sworn it was mine." He drew his sword, a fine looking weapon of obviously superior craftsmanship.

"I guess there's only one way to find out," he said calmly.

Scott stepped between the thief and William,

"If you want to hurt Will, you'll have to go through me first" he growled.

The thief said nothing; he simply raised his blade and prepared to fight.

"Who are you?" Jon asked, he was a bit confused by all of this.

The thief reached up and tossed back his hood, and shock registered on the faces of the rest of the group. The young man before them looked exactly like Scott. The same intelligent, aristocratic features and blue grey eyes. The only noticeable difference being the thief's single lock of white hair while Scott's was entirely brown in color.

"My name is Isaac," said the look-alike.

*   *   *

Everyone stared dumbfounded. David however only smiled and looked at Scott and Isaac thoughtfully.

"Hmm," he said quietly, "that's interesting."

*   *   *

Scott raised his sword and growled at the young stranger,

"I don't know who you are," he said, "but you're not getting your hands on this book."

"I'm afraid I can't allow that," said Isaac. He made a saluting motion with his sword and leaped forward on the attack. Scott stepped to the side and brought his own sword up to parry Isaac's, then whirled around and made a swift overhand chop. Isaac brought his sword overhead and stopped Scott's blade, then slipped to the right and thrust his blade at his opponent's torso.

* * *

Off to the side Scott's friends were watching the two young swordsmen.

"Wow," said Loki, assessing the spectacle, "they're good."

"Yeah," agreed Jon, "but Scott's definitely stronger."

"True," said David, "but Isaac has much better form."

* * *

Scott narrowly avoided Isaac's thrust and deflected the look-alike boy's sword aside. Isaac carried the motion around; he twirled around elegantly before flicking the tip of his blade across Scott's left shoulder.

* * *

"Is he sword fighting or dancing?" asked William,

"Some fencing disciplines are very similar to dance," said Jon, "it's often really cool to watch."

* * *

Scott roared in pain from his cut shoulder and attacked his opponent savagely. His big sword flicked this way and that, its speed belying the blade's weight and size. Isaac was hard pressed to block the rapid slashes. Scott managed to strike a single hit, cutting a line of deep crimson across Isaac's chest. Isaac let out a yell and staggered back, his features twisted in a snarl. He wiped his hand across his chest and stared at the blood.

Scott assumed a fighting stance and smiled,

"Care to try again?" he asked.

Isaac leaped forward with a wordless snarl, sword high above his head. Scott stepped back and held up his blade. Isaac's attack made a loud clang as it struck Scott's sword. Scott pushed Isaac away and spun around to attack Isaac's right side. The young man skillfully parried the blow and stepped to the left. He made a swift, upward cut with his blade. Scott raised his arm out of harm's way and ended up getting a vertical gash across his right eye.

He dropped his sword and clutched both hands to his eye. He doubled over in pain, looking up at Isaac as the blood from the cut streaked across his face. Isaac raised his sword and assumed a ready stance. Scott bared his teeth and let out a growl. He grabbed up his sword, charged forward and attacked. There was no time for Isaac to react. Scott's attack caught him across the left eye, giving him a cut that mirrored his own. The young man fell backward onto the stone floor.

Scott stood over him, sword point to his throat.

"So," he asked, "are you going to leave? Or do I have to kill you?"

Isaac stared at his opponent through the blood from his wound, his face in an expression of rage and defiance.

"Fine," he said, "keep the book, but you'll regret starting this fight. If we meet again one of us will not live to see the sun go down." He picked himself up and ran down a side corridor before hopping out a window.

Scott watched him go, the cuts on his shoulder and face still bleeding. He turned to the group, sheathed his sword and walked toward them.

"Are you okay?" asked Isis, her voice fraught with concern.

"I'm...fine," said Scott. He then collapsed on the floor.

Isis ran to him and knelt down.

"What happened?" she asked.

"Blood loss," shouted David. "We have to find him a doctor."

They all lifted their injured friend and carried him out the door and into the night.

*   *   *

Meanwhile, Jessia, James and Krant were struggling to haul their loot out the window of the castle.

"You filled the bags up too much," admonished Krant, "they won't fit through with the way you stuffed them with gold."

"Well you're the one who found all that gold," shot back James. "I never would have filled the bags that much if you hadn't found so much to put in them."

"Both of you shut up," commanded Jessia, "Someone's coming."

The door to the room opened and three men stepped through. Two were large, armor clad guards; the third was a small, wiry man in a long blue robe: Malagent.

"They must have gone this way," Malagent said, "search the room for the assassins."

The first thing that the trio noticed was the thieves. The guards immediately drew their swords and assumed an attack stance. James screamed and Krant shoved the bag out of the window, Jessia drew her own sword.

Malagent appeared to take control,

"Well," he said, "it looks like we have a nest of rats in the castle." He snapped his fingers twice and pointed at the thieves,

"Show them what we do with vermin gentlemen," he told the guards. As Malagent turned to walk out the door as the guards stepped forward with their swords gripped tightly.

Krant quickly formed an escape plan in his mind, but he needed a diversion "Jessia," he said, "hold them off while I find a way to get us out of here."

Jessia stepped up to the guards and raised her blade to attack. The guards hesitated for a moment; they had never encountered a female swordfighter. Jessia took the opportunity and leaped forward with a battle cry taking on both at once.

James watched as Jessia fought with the two guards. Krant came up and grabbed him by the ear,

"Come on," said Krant, "I'm going to need your help with this."

They grabbed the drapery from around the room and knotted it together. When they had a piece of sufficient length Krant tied it to the curtain rod over the window.

"Jessia," he shouted, "time to get the hell out of here."

Jessia ran from her opponents to the window as James and Krant slid down the makeshift rope to the ground. As soon as Jessia touched the ground, the trio gathered what loot they had gotten out of the castle and ran as far away as they could.

Episode II
A Fallen Friend

CHAPTER ONE:
Three Weeks

Scott's eyes snapped open. Correction, only one *eye*, his left eye to be precise. He brought his hand to the right side of his face and felt gauzy fabric, bandages. There were more bandages across his shoulder. Where am I? he wondered. He sat up, rather painfully, and took stock of his situation. He was lying on a fairly comfortable bed in a plainly appointed room built from light colored sandstone. There were several other beds in the room, all empty. Bandages on face… room full of beds…I must be in a hospital of some kind, he thought, guess my friends brought me here.

"Ah," said a voice, "you're awake."

Scott looked in the direction of the voice and saw a young man in brown wool robes, probably a monk.

"Your friends will be glad to know you're all right, I will bring them."

He put his hands together in a blessing, bowed his head and left.

Scott sat back and closed his eye, and let the sounds of this new place come to him. The soft tread of sandals on the stone floor, the twittering and chirping of birds outside, the clattering of dishes in the kitchen. Then Scott heard a new sound, the footsteps of all his friends. He sensed Jon's over-confident swagger, Loki's cautious soft stepping, Isis and Katherine's graceful strides and William's intrepid paces. There was also a set of steps he didn't recognize. They were somewhat heavy, with a steady rhythm of pace which indicated they belonged to a large, strong person with plenty of dignity and nobility. Scott wondered who this person could be until the door opened to reveal his friends and a big man with close cropped hair and beard shot through with gray. The stranger wore wire-rimmed spectacles and robes of the same color as the monk he had seen earlier, but with a white trim around the hem, which Scott guessed meant he was an official in the order.

"So," asked Scott as he sat up, "how bad is it?"

"Your wound has been treated young warrior," said the old monk,

"However," he added solemnly, "The damage to your right eye was irreparable. There was nothing I could do."

Scott swore and slammed his fist into the bedpost.

"How are you feeling man?" his friends asked.

"Fine considering," he replied pointing to his bandages, "How long was I out?"

"Three days," said Katherine. "After your fight at the castle David had us bring you here and Mortimer treated your wounds."

"Mortimer?" said Scott with a raised eyebrow.

"That would be me," said the old man, "Mortimer Stormcrow, Abbot of Redstone Abbey."

"Well thanks," said Scott, "come on guys, let's find David and let's go." He started to get up, and fell right back down.

Mortimer smiled, "I'm afraid you won't be going very far in your condition young man," he said.

"Besides," said William, "David left right after we got here."

Scott swore loudly and punched the head board of the bed causing it to splinter.

Mortimer whistled, "My, my," he said, "you are quite a strong young man." He left the room chuckling softly. Scott tried standing up again, this time he managed to stay up by grabbing the edge of the bed.

"So," he asked, "where did David go?"

"He said he was going to find a way off the island," said William.

"A way off the island?" asked Scott.

"Yeah," said Jon, "he said it was a ship or something."

How typical of Jon to not pay attention, thought Scott.

Loki stepped forward with a stout walking stick in his hands and offered it to Scott.

"Here," he said, "David said it might help."

"Thanks," said Scott. He held the staff in his hand feeling its weight. It was nearly as tall as himself and made of strong, well-weathered oak. It felt very comfortable in his hand. He leaned on it heavily as he walked around the room. It supported him just fine, but there was just one more thing to test. He popped it into the air, he tried to grab it but missed and it clattered on the floor. He tried again, this time he caught it at just about mid-length and knocked on the back of Loki's head. It made a hollow clunk sound.

"Ow!" said Loki as he rubbed the back of his head.

"Works perfectly," pronounced Scott with a slight smile. He walked over to a pack beside his bed and opened it. Inside were several sets of clothes. He removed a tan colored tunic and pulled it on over his head. He stretched his arms out wide, his back and shoulders cracking loudly.

"Well," he said, "if we can't leave yet, we might as well make ourselves at home." They all walked out of the infirmary, William made sure to grab the pack before he left.

*   *   *

Isis walked up close to Scott as he made his way down the corridor. She leaned her head against his shoulder and tucked her arm inside his. The two of them stepped into a side corridor, and their friends kept walking to give them some privacy.

"I'm glad you're better," she said coyly, "I was getting lonely."

"Me too," replied Scott. He ran his fingers through her hair and kissed her on the mouth.

"Come on," she said, "let me show you around."

*   *   *

The group walked into the Great Hall after Scott and Isis left.

"I still don't know how they got together," said Loki.

"I do," said Katherine, "She's the only one he shows any kind of emotion to."

"What do you mean?" asked Loki.

"Come on Loki," said Jon, "you've seen the two of them together. When Isis is around Scott is like a completely different person." It was true, Scott usually had a very uptight personality but when he was with Isis he softened significantly. He would even smile for her, something he rarely did for anyone else.

"I guess so," conceded Loki, "so what are we going to do while the love birds are busy?"

"Well," said William, "I suppose we could see what there is to do around here."

"Good idea Will," said Katherine, "as a matter of fact I saw some people playing cards over near the kitchen." They left the room and explored their new home for the next several weeks.

*   *   *

William walked through the corridors admiring the building and its grounds. The place was beautiful. Red sandstone buildings surrounded by lovingly tended orchards and gardens. There was a general air of peace and calm over the entire place and William felt right at home. He walked out into the garden and sat down under a tree. The warm summer breeze carried the scent of flowers in the air. It reminded him very much of his mother's beloved rose garden. Gradually he found that his eyes couldn't stay open. I suppose I could take a nap I suppose, he thought. So he closed his eyes, leaned his head back and fell asleep.

"Excuse me," the voice snapped him out of his nap in an instant. He looked up to see who was speaking, a young monk in baggy robes and sandals that were far too large for him.

"What is it?" asked William.

"Abbot Mortimer would like to see you," said the monk.

"Okay" said William. He stood up and followed the young man back into the Abbey. He was lead through the corridors to the Abbot's rectory. The young monk knocked four times and then waited for a response.

"Enter," came the slightly muffled response from within. The monk opened the door and escorted William inside. Abbot Mortimer was seated in a very comfortable looking armchair reading a book.

"Thank you Matthias," he said to the monk. The young man bowed respectfully and closed the door behind him.

"Please have a seat William," said Mortimer gesturing to a chair next to his own. William sank himself into the chair and turned to the Abbot,

"What did you want to see me about?" he asked.

Mortimer rose from his chair and put his book back on the shelf,

"You are the book keeper are you not?" he asked William.

William cocked an eyebrow at that,

"Book keeper?" he asked.

"You are in possession of the Book of Power correct?" asked the Abbot.

"Yes," said William, a bit cautious after the encounter with Isaac. Mortimer nodded,

"Keep that book safe young man," he warned, "in the wrong hands that book can bring about terrible destruction."

"What do you mean?"

"You don't know?" said Mortimer incredulously, "Well, I suppose I envy you for that," he continued.

"Why?" asked William.

"Because throughout the ages there have been individuals who would do anything to obtain great power," said the Abbot, "the Book of Power is literally that, tangible power. I'm sure you've read some of the spells contained within its pages."

"Yes," said William his hand involuntarily grabbed the book protectively in his satchel.

"Don't worry young man," said Mortimer, "I have no need for it. I am a scholar, not a conqueror."

William allowed himself to relax. He removed his hands from the book and set them in his lap.

"May I see the book William?" asked Mortimer. William took the book out of his bag and set it down on the small table between the two chairs. Mortimer sat back down and picked up the book. He turned it over in his hands several times, a look of reminiscence upon his weathered features.

"It has been a long time since I last looked upon this book. I thought it was gone forever, David and I made sure of that."

"You knew David?" said William in astonishment.

"Yes," said Mortimer, "David and I were once the guardians of the book's original keepers. But then evil tried to take the book, so we hid it away where no one could find it, your world."

"How?" asked William.

"You've read the book," said Mortimer, "you know what sort things you can do with the spells written inside."

"Couldn't you just have destroyed it?"

"No. The powers locked away in that book protect it from destruction. The only thing we could do was hide it."

"What happened to the book's original keepers?" asked William.

"That is something not even David and I know," replied Mortimer "They disappeared along with the book."

"What happened?" asked William.

"It all started about fourteen years ago," began Mortimer, "back then, David and I were servants to the king of Veridea. A powerful lord and good friend of the king betrayed him and staged a coup. He stormed the capitol and tried to take the book by force. We managed to escape from his army and get to safety. The last time either of us saw them was right after we sent the book away."

"Well," said William, "maybe they went with the book."

"Perhaps," said Mortimer, his eyes had a sly twinkle as he answered. William got the feeling that Mortimer did know what happened but wasn't going to tell.

"Didn't you try to find them?" asked William.

"If we tried to the king's enemies would follow us to them," said Mortimer, "we decided it was for the best if they remained lost."

"Thank you for telling me about the book," said William, "I'll keep in mind what you told me." He rose from his chair and turned towards the door.

"Remember William," said Mortimer, "if used improperly that book may cause unspeakable destruction." William left the room and walked back to the garden and finished his nap under the tree.

*   *   *

Hidden in the woods across the road from the Abbey was a small ramshackle camp occupied by a trio of thieves: Jessia, James and Krant.

"Why do we have to do this?" Krant asked James.

"Because," said James, "We used up all the gold from the castle trying to get here. So we need to get more and they're bound to have some at least."

"But why an Abbey?" asked Krant.

"Well," said James, "it's nearby and unguarded. It will be a piece of cake to steal from a bunch of foolish monks." He sounded fairly confident in his "master plan." Krant felt otherwise however, he was very familiar with Redstone Abbey; the monks there may be peaceful but would not hesitate to defend themselves from intruders. Many a thief had found themselves sent down the road bandaged up and in authoritative custody after attempting to rob the Abbey. He wasn't too keen on becoming a member of that club.

"So James," said Jessia, "why don't you run us through your plan again?" she asked.

"It's simple," said James, "one of us sneaks into the Abbey, searches around for wherever they keep the gold and get back out with a decent amount of it."

"And how much do you figure is 'a decent amount'?" asked Krant.

James thought a bit and said,

"About a pound or two should do."

Krant nodded in agreement, Jessia also had a question,

"How do you know they even have gold in there?" she asked.

"There has to be," declared James, "monks always gives alms gold to the poor, they have to keep a stock of it some where in there."

"All right," conceded Krant, "I'll check the Abbey out for gold, but if this plan backfires on us James. You'll be very sorry."

"Okay," said James, "but what will you do Jessia?" he asked.

"I was going to see if there was anything to steal in the town down the road," replied Jessia.

The three thieves clasped their hands together and then separated to prepare for their respective jobs.

*   *   *

After Isis had finished showing him around the Abbey she had gone back to her room, leaving Scott to wander the hallways by himself. At this particular moment he was following his nose to the wonderful smells of the kitchen. As he passed by he heard a soft thrumming sound, the sound of sword being swung. Looking to the source of the sound Scott found Jon Belmont practicing with his blade. Jon held the sword with a natural ease, his hands spaced apart on the long handgrip. Scott leaned on his staff quietly and watched his friend practice thrusts, coups and ripostes, each maneuver seamlessly blending into the next. Finally, Scott decided to pass a comment on the show.

"Not bad Jon," he assessed.

Jon turned suddenly, nearly dropping his sword in the process. He spotted Scott and wiped the sweat from his brow with a grin.

"Figured I'd get a little practice in before you recover and whip my ass" he said.

Scott laughed.

"And what makes you think that?" he asked.

"I did watch your fight with Isaac you know," replied Jon, "there's no way I could stand up to skill like that. So I asked David to teach me how to use a sword."

"Hmm," said Scott, "David seems to be a multi-talented guy."

"I'll say," said Jon. "The first sparring match we had, I was flat on my butt before I even knew what happened."

"Wow!" exclaimed Scott. Jon was normally very quick to react.

"So how do you think I did?" asked Jon.

"Not bad," said Scott, "you still need a bit of work on your form, but otherwise you're pretty good."

"What about you?" asked Jon, "Where do you learn how to use a sword?"

"I don't really know," Scott confessed, "it just comes to me naturally, like I always knew how to do it. Kind of weird isn't it."

"Yeah," agreed Jon, "it is a little strange. I guess I should get back to practicing."

Scott let Jon resume his fencing practice and continued down the corridor to the kitchen. His nose caught a whiff of something delicious, homemade shepherd's pie. Scott ran toward the smell as fast as someone with a walking stick can run.

* * *

That evening William was out in the garden engaging in one of his favorite pastimes: stargazing. He had always loved looking at the night sky. Back on Earth he could find all of the stars and constellations there were to see. Here however, on this new and unfamiliar world of Midaria, the sky was filled with two moons, unknown stars and constellations he had never known.

True, there was no light pollution like there was in all but the most northern parts of Michigan, but there was none of the comfort that he felt in the night here. He didn't have the feeling of familiarity that knowing the night sky so well brought to him. Oh well, he thought, I guess I can learn everything about the constellations here too. He put anymore troubling thoughts from his mind and let his eyes roam across the patch of the cosmos that hung over the garden. Then he noticed something familiar, a single constellation that looked almost identical to the ones on Earth. In fact, it was one of the ones on Earth, but the constellation appeared to be backwards (at least from his perspective) and the brightest stars were entirely different. This started a train of thought in William's mind. This discovery could help him find out how far away they had come from home, and maybe, just maybe, it might also provide a clue to getting home.

CHAPTER TWO:
Mealtime Surprise

The next morning started fairly normal for Jon Belmont. He woke up, ate a breakfast of scrambled eggs and pastries prepared in the Abbey kitchen, and then chatted with Scott in the Abbey Library.

"What are you reading?" Jon asked.

"Believe it or not Isaac Asimov," said Scott blinking in bewilderment.

"How is that possible?" asked Jon in the same tone. After all, they were on another world; there was no way that a book from Earth should be there.

"I don't know," said Scott, "maybe they have their own Asimov." It wasn't a very scientific explanation, but it would do for the moment.

"So," asked Jon, "are you feeling any better?"

"A little," replied Scott, "Mortimer said all I need is rest for the time being."

Jon sat down on the chair next to Scott's and looked at his friend with a smile.

"How did we get ourselves into this?" he asked.

"Who knows," said Scott. "Maybe this was supposed to happen to us." His eyes looked somewhere far away.

"How do you figure that?" asked Jon.

"I don't know," said Scott, "it just feels that way."

Jon didn't understand that but went along with it anyway. Scott had this funny habit of being right most of the time.

"Okay man," he said, "whatever you say."

Scott got up out of his chair and limped over to the book shelf to put his book back.

"Where are you going?" asked Jon.

"I was just going to walk around for a bit," said Scott. "Find something else to do."

Jon joined his friend and helped him out of the library by opening the door,

"I think I saw Loki over in the gardens," he said. "Maybe we could play cards or something."

"Sounds good," agreed Scott. They walked out to the gardens to find Loki.

* * *

Isis woke up that morning to find a surprising development in her bathroom mirror: a single lock of her hair had turned pure white.

Quite naturally, she was shocked to discover this. She let out a shriek which immediately brought a concerned Katherine to her door.

"What's wrong?" she asked.

"Look," said Isis indicating her hair.

Katherine's eyes widened in surprise.

"Whoa," she said, "that's different."

"No kidding," said Isis.

"Any idea how it happened?" asked Katherine.

"No," said Isis. "What is Scott going to think?"

Katherine didn't know how to respond to that. Isis seemed to notice this,

"I'm sorry," she said, "I guess I'm feeling a little scared right now."

"Do you have any idea what caused this?" asked Katherine.

"No," said Isis, "I think I'll talk to Mortimer. He'll probably know something about it."

* * *

Some distance down the road from the Abbey, a lone figure in a black cloak limped down the path using a long branch broken off a dead tree as a crutch.

Isaac looked back behind him; he could still see the roof of the Abbey over the trees. He had spotted the group from the castle at the Abbey and left as soon as he could, while he fully intended to fulfill the promise he'd made at the castle he was not in any shape to do so physically. No matter though, as soon as he was back to full strength he would find the young man he battled at the castle and fulfill his promise. He turned his eyes forward and continued on his way. Then he heard the sound of footsteps coming up behind him. He guessed they belonged to some other traveler. He politely stepped aside to let them pass and noticed that the person walking behind him was one of the thieves he had met that night. He ducked his head low so that she couldn't see his face. In his current state, she might see him fit as a target to rob and he was definitely in no condition to defend himself. She walked past him oblivious to his identity. He watched her until she was out of sight and continued down the road.

*   *   *

"I can't believe I let you talk me into this," complained Krant as he and James sat at the base of the Abbey Wall.

"Well you said it was good yesterday," said James.

"No I didn't," clarified Krant, "I said I'd go along with it so long as it didn't get us into trouble."

James nodded in agreement,

"Okay," he conceded, "you did say that. But we're still going through with the plan."

"Fine," said Krant, "but I still don't think this is a good idea."

"Why?" asked James.

"Because," said Krant, "better thieves than us have tried to rob this place and every single one has ended up being sent to jail by the monks."

"Oh," said James, suddenly noticing a hole in his "perfect" plan. "I didn't know that."

"Well if you weren't so confident in your plan yesterday I would've had time to tell you," admonished Krant, "but you didn't seem to want to listen."

"Sorry," said James, "but it's too late. We can't go back now."

"Really," said Krant with a raised eyebrow.

"Yeah," said James, "we're already here. It wouldn't be right to stop."

"Really," said Krant with a sarcastic smile.

"Just get up the wall old man," urged James.

Krant scratched the iron gray scruff on his chin,

"Who are you calling old?" he said to his apprentice.

"Okay I'm sorry," said James, "just climb up the wall."

"All right," said Krant, "I'm going." He wriggled his fingers into the cracks between the stone blocks and climbed rapidly up the wall. He jumped down into some bushes on the other side and looked around to see if anyone had spotted him. The area was clear so he stealthily made his way over to an open window and checked inside. No one was there. He squeezed through the narrow window and fell to the floor. He picked himself up with a groan and dusted off his vest. He looked around for valuables, but there was nothing. He was in what appeared to be a laundry room. Well, he thought, this could still be useful. He picked up a robe that looked about his size, put it on and headed to other parts of the Abbey.

*   *   *

William was sitting in the room he'd been given working on a project he'd begun the night before when a soft knock came from his door. He and opened the door to find brother Matthias waiting patiently.

"Hello Matthias," said William, "what brings you here?" he asked.

"Your friends wanted to know what you were doing," said Matthias. "You've been in here all morning."

"I have?" asked William.

"Yes," replied Matthias, "they thought you'd overslept."

"No I didn't." William told the monk, "I was just working on something."

"What were you working on?" asked the young monk. He looked around the room, finally noticing the papers taped all over the walls and covered with William's hasty scrawl.

"Oh, it's nothing," said William, "just a little math problem."

"Little?" asked Matthias incredulously.

William chuckled,

"Well," he said, "maybe I did get a little carried away."

"So what is your problem about?" asked Matthias.

William sat back down in the chair and began his explanation,

"Well," he said," I was out in the gardens last night stargazing when I noticed that one of your world's constellations looks the same as one we have on Earth. We call it 'Orion the Hunter' but the one here is 'The Noble King'."

"How did you know that?" asked Matthias.

"I asked one of your brother monks," said William, "Anyway the constellations are almost identical. Yours is smaller and backwards, but otherwise the same as the one on Earth. That got me thinking that I could find out where your world is in relation to mine and so...." He gestured with his hands to indicate his work.

Matthias shook his head and whistled.

"I didn't understand a word of what you just said," he said, "but I do understand that it's important to you."

"Thanks," said William.

"You know," said Matthias, "maybe you should take a break."

"Yeah," agreed William, "I think I should."

"I saw some of your friends heading out to the gardens, perhaps you should join them."

"Thanks," said William, "I will."

Matthias and William left the room and parted ways. William headed toward the gardens and Matthias went off to continue his daily chores. On his way he passed a fellow monk who was trying very hard to shield his face from view.

"Excuse me," he said, "but may I help you?"

The other man stiffened suddenly, like someone had strapped an iron bar to his spine,

"I'm fine," he said in a voice that sounded like a cat's screech, "I was just looking for the gardener. I passed through the garden and happened to notice that some of the bushes are in need of pruning, I simply wished to inform him of this."

"Okay," said Matthias, inwardly suspicious of this stranger. The gardeners went to work early every morning and tended their plants until sundown. If the other monk was looking for the gardener, he would already have found him.

"I believe he's over by the gate tending the roses," he continued, "I'm sure he'll be glad to know." He kept walking, but instead of heading to his chores, went to tell the Abbot of the intruder. He would be able to find out who this stranger was.

*   *   *

Krant breathed a sigh of relief as the young monk in ill-fitting robes and sandals left. The cover story he'd given seemed to have worked so he continued looking for things to steal. He inspected an ornate woven tapestry hanging on the wall. It was no doubt valuable, but it was far too large to remove without help and he'd probably be noticed if he tried to carry the colossal piece of fabric out of the Abbey. Personally he doubted that he would find anything that would satisfy James, but you never know, he thought, there are hidden treasures around every turn.

*   *   *

Scott, William, Jon and Loki were sitting on the flagstones in the gardens playing a game of Euchre with a deck of cards that Jon had picked up in the town down the road. So far Loki and William were winning.

"They've got to be cheating, man," Jon was telling Scott, "there's just no way he could win thirteen hands in a row."

Scott looked at him quizzically,

"And the fact that you're a horrible Euchre player doesn't factor into that statement."

"Hey!" said Jon, "it was your idea to play this game."

"Because I expected you to be a better player," retorted Scott.

"Shut up!" Jon shot back. "I still think they're counting cards."

"That's in Blackjack, Jon," said Loki and William.

Jon grumbled something about lousy cheaters and laid down his card, a ten of diamonds. Loki immediately trumped Jon's card with the King of Clubs. William, expecting he and his partner to win yet another hand put down the nine of diamonds.

"Not bad guys," said Scott, "but I think I'll take this one." He set down, the Right Bower, the highest card in the game. Loki's jaw dropped as Scott collected the hand and placed them off to the side.

"What's the matter Loki?" he asked politely, "you look upset."

"I don't believe it," said Loki, "I stacked the deck perfectly."

"I knew it!" shouted Jon, "you were cheating!"

"Only a little," said Loki trying hard to look as innocent as possible. The two of them glared at each other with looks that could have knocked down a brick wall. Fortunately, Scott sensed the tension between his friends and decided to prevent it from going further. Though Jon and Loki's fights were often quite hilarious, this was neither the time nor the place for one.

"I'm done with this game," he said quickly, "let's do something else."

"Like what?" asked William.

"Well," said Scott, "it is almost lunch time and I have something special planned that I think you guys will love."

*   *   *

The "something special" that Scott had planned turned out to be a cooking contest between himself and Hugo, the Abbey's Head Cook. Apparently Scott's visit to the kitchens the night before had included him taking the place over and making dinner for the monks. Hugo had decided to see which one was the better cook and proposed the contest. Loki, William and Jon had been assigned as judges. The two contenders went straight to work, laboring long and hard to create the most perfect meal. Hugo's dish was fresh fish from the Abbey pond, grilled to perfection in lemon-pepper and garlic served with sautéed mushrooms and a mixed green salad with homemade dressing. Scott cooked a meal of grilled white meat chicken liberally coated with white sauce and a special blend of spices followed by squash soup and a balsamic vinaigrette. After much deliberation, some arguing and a second and third helping the judges decided to vote Scott's as the better meal.

"That's alright Hugo," said Scott, "I'm not trying to take your job."

"Besides," he whispered, "just between us. My friends are a little biased, they aren't really the types for fine dining."

Hugo laughed.

"They aren't at that," he said, "they wouldn't know good food if you stuffed it down their gullets." The two culinary artists burst out laughing.

"Tell you what," said Hugo, "even though you don't want my job, you can come in here any time and cook whatever takes your fancy."

"Thank you," said Scott, not knowing what else to say.

"Well then," said Hugo cheerfully, "dinner is all yours. So if you'll excuse me, I'll be getting to some nice fishing in the Abbey pond."

Scott set to work immediately with the other cooks preparing dinner for the evening. Hugo went off to the pond and sat in his favorite fishing spot under the shade of a willow tree. Dinner was absolutely delicious, however Loki, Jon and William were not in attendance, apparently they were asleep digesting after their role in the contest.

*   *   *

After dinner Scott and Isis sat in the garden and talked about Isis' sudden change of hairstyle.

"Do you know what caused it?" Scott asked.

"Mortimer said it's because I apparently have magical ability," said Isis.

"Well," said Scott, "that would explain the things that happened at the castle."

Isis twirled the lock of white hair in her fingers and looked at her boy friend,

"How do you think it looks?" she asked.

Scott looked at the white hair on her brow; it was a definite contrast to her soft, black tresses, but it wasn't hideous. He thought it made her more beautiful. Something he previously hadn't thought possible.

"I think it looks just fine," he told her.

"You really think so?" she said.

"Of course," he said, "I think it looks beautiful."

That made her feel much better. Scott always knew what to say to make her feel better. It was one of the many things she loved about him. She immediately threw her arms around him and kissed him softly.

"Thanks," she said and headed off to her room.

*   *   *

The next morning, the residents and guests of Redstone Abbey were treated to the best breakfast ever to come out of the kitchens. This was only fitting seeing as both Scott and Hugo had prepared it. All of Scott's friends sat down at a table and waited for the Abbot to say the blessing. After that, breakfast was served: raspberry and cinnamon pancakes with a vegetarian omelet, hash browns and lots of syrup. Brother Matthias wheeled the beverage cart around serving milk, coffee and tea. The dining hall very quickly filled with the chatter of several dozen conversations and the clatter of plates. After making his rounds Matthias sat down between Jon and Loki and served himself.

"This is the best meal I've ever had," he reported.

"Scott's meals usually are," said Katherine.

"Yeah," said Loki, "I've never met anyone who could cook better than Scott."

"Where's Will been?" asked Isis. "I haven't seen him since yesterday."

"He's in his room," answered Matthias, "working on some math problem."

"What kind of math problem?" asked Katherine.

"When I asked him about it I didn't understand a word of what he said."

"Will has a tendency to do that," said Loki to everyone's laughter.

Matthias took a moment to look around the room.

"Where did Scott go?" he asked.

"Back in the kitchen," said Isis.

"Already?" asked Matthias, it seemed odd to him that he wouldn't come out to eat with his friends."

"Scott probably helped himself to breakfast as he was cooking it," Katherine told him, "he calls it 'quality control'."

"Besides Matti," said Loki, "the longer Scott is in the kitchen, the better the meal. Trust me."

Matthias looked at the lanky thief coyly,

"I wouldn't trust you if my life depended on it," he said.

"Wise move," said Jon.

Everyone else laughed, Loki made an exaggerated pout.

"I wonder what lunch is going to be?" asked Isis off-handedly.

Katherine suddenly had a strange expression on her face; her eyes seemed to stare off into the distance.

"Roasted chicken in red sauce with spinach and watercress soup," she said.

"How do you know that?" asked Matthias.

Katherine blinked suddenly, "I don't know," she said, "I just saw it."

Jon cocked an eyebrow strangely, "What do you mean?" he asked his sister.

"I can't really explain it," said Katherine, "it was like I could see all of us sitting here having lunch, but it hasn't happened yet."

"Okay," said Jon, "that's a little weird."

"Hey Matti," asked Loki, "Are all of the monks in the Abbey here?"

"I think so," said Matthias, "Why do you ask?"

"Because I saw someone in monk's robes walking around casing the place," said Loki.

"Casing?" asked Matthias. He was unfamiliar with Loki's slang terms.

"He means looking for stuff to steal," said Jon.

"Why would someone want to steal from the Abbey," asked Katherine.

"I don't know," said Jon, "but I'm going to find out. Come on Loki," he called. Loki looked longingly at his plate as Jon lead him out of the room and down the hall.

*   *   *

Krant made his way as stealthily as possible toward the kitchen. After spending the night sleeping in a closet he was hungry for a decent breakfast. The smells from the kitchen were intoxicating and he got hungrier with every step. Suddenly he heard voices coming down the hall. He peeked around a corner to see who it was; two young men came down the hall conversing amiably. One was tall and lanky with a messy shock of brown hair; the other was of more average height with short cropped blond hair. Krant quickly assessed the two boys; if he had to fight them he could probably take the taller one. The other had muscles thick as tree limbs, but didn't look too bright, so it would be better to outsmart him. As Krant peeked at them from around the corner the two boys stopped talking and looked around,

"Hey Jon," asked the taller one, "Do you feel like we're being watched?"

"Yes I do, Loki," replied Jon, "I really do."

Krant quickly pulled his head from around the corner and stiffened up against the fall, hoping they wouldn't find him. Unfortunately for Krant, Jon and Loki were a lot more observant than most people gave them credit for. Krant felt a strong pair of hands grab his shoulders and pull him back into the hallway. Jon and Loki surveyed their catch.

"Well, well," said Jon, "looks like we found a thief."

"I do believe you're right," agreed Loki.

Krant immediately ripped off his disguise and threw the torn fabric at his captors. He took off down the hall as fast as his feet would carry him.

Unfortunately, he wasn't a very fast runner and Loki and Jon easily caught up with him. They pinned him up against the wall and held him there.

"What were you looking for in here?" demanded Jon.

"Oh nothing special," said Krant, "a little of this, a little of that."

"Yeah right," said Loki, "hand over whatever you took and we'll let you go."

"I didn't take anything," blurted Krant, "I swear."

Jon and Loki didn't believe him.

"Search him," said Jon.

Loki patted Krant down and turned out the various pockets on his vest, but all he found was a set of lock picks, a rag, a bottle of oil and a very shiny copper coin that Krant considered a good luck charm: basic tools for any thief. Loki put everything back in Krant's pockets and let go of him.

"Well Jon," said Loki, "he was telling the truth. He didn't take anything."

"So does that mean you're going to let me go?" asked Krant.

"Yeah," said Jon with an unnerving grin, "we'll let you go."

* * *

Jon and Loki took the would-be robber and dragged him to the abbey's main gate. After having the gate-keepers open it they took the thief by the belt and shirt collar and hurled him out into the road. Jon waved good bye as the gate closed,

"Don't come back now," he said with mocking pleasantry, "you hear."

"Well," said Loki, "that takes care of him."

"That it does," said Jon, "what do you say we go find the girls and get a card game going. I could use the practice."

"Careful Jon," warned Loki. "Isis is a bigger card-shark than I am."

The two boys headed back into the Abbey laughing.

* * *

James ran out of the woods when he saw Krant thrown out of the Abbey gate.

"Are you all right?" he asked the older man.

"No thanks to you," retorted Krant. "I knew your plan wouldn't work."

"What do you mean?" asked James.

"Not only was there nothing to steal," said Krant, "but there are some travelers in the Abbey that have taken upon themselves to toss any innocent thief they catch out the door."

"Well how was I supposed to know that there were other people in the Abbey?" said James.

Krant smacked the young thief on the back of the head.

"You could try looking around next time," he admonished. "Scouting out a place before you go inside and steal things will let you learn the habits of any occupants."

James rubbed the sore spot with a guilty look on his face.

"Okay," he said, "I'll remember next time."

"You'd better," warned Krant, "or there might not be a next time."

"Are you boys finished arguing, or do I have to finish it for you," said Jessia as she walked up to her two companions.

"How did your job go?" Krant asked her.

"See for yourself," she replied, holding up two large sacks that jingled musically.

"Well," said Krant, "it's nice to know at least one of you knows what you're doing." He gave James a foul look.

"Now," continued Krant, "let's head into town and see what other valuables we can obtain."

"I like that idea," said James, "wait until you hear my plan to get inside the mayor's mansion."

Krant hit him again.

"I've about had enough of your plans James," he said. "We're going to do this my way."

The three thieves walked down the road into town as Krant outlined *his* plan to rob the mayor.

*   *   *

Jon had decided to take a walk around the Abbey while Loki went looking for Isis and Katherine. As he strolled down a shady cloister he heard the familiar flip-flop of over sized sandals.

"Hello Matthias," he said.

"How'd you know it was me?" asked the young monk.

"Your sandals are about three sizes too big for your feet Matthias," said Jon, "maybe you should get a pair that actually fits."

"These were all they had," said Matthias.

"That's too bad," said Jon. "Maybe you could get a pair in town."

"Maybe I could," said Matthias, "I heard that Scott was going into town later to get a special surprise for dinner this evening."

"Sounds cool," said Jon.

"Hey Jon," asked Matthias, "Why doesn't Loki call most people by their names?"

"That's just Loki," said Jon. "He likes giving people nicknames. I guess he finds them easier to remember."

"Okay," said Matthias. He started to move away nervously.

"You know, Matthias," said Jon, "you don't have to be afraid of me." The young monk had always acted a little nervous around him.

"I'm not afraid of you," said Matthias. "You're bigger than me, that's all."

"Really," said Jon.

"Well," admitted Matthias, "you do have kind of a sour disposition."

"I do not!" said Jon.

"Yes you do, Jon," said a voice. It was Scott.

"That sounds a lot like the pot calling the kettle black," Jon told his friend.

"I definitely don't have a sour disposition," said Scott.

"Yes," said Matthias, "it's much more uptight."

Jon had to admit, that the statement described Scott almost exactly. Scott chuckled softly.

"Thank you Matthias," he said pleasantly.

"Aren't you supposed to be making lunch?" asked Jon.

"Already did," said Scott, "it just needs to be served."

"Oh," said Jon, "so what do you say we go have some."

"Sounds like a good idea," said Matthias.

The three young men headed to the dining hall to have lunch. It was exactly what Katherine said it would be.

* * *

Isis and Katherine were feeling rather bored. True the Abbey was beautiful, but even beauty becomes boring if you spend too much time around it. So they elected for a change of scenery by heading into town for the day. However, they needed permission from the Abbot to go into town. The girls went out into the hallways and headed to Mortimer's rectory. They found him reading in his armchair as usual. They told him their idea,

"The town is a very rough place," he told them, "I would hate to see you young ladies get hurt."

"We won't go alone," said Isis.

Mortimer gave her a funny look over the top of his spectacles; it made him look very parentish. He sat back in his chair, stroking his beard thoughtfully.

"Very well," he said at last, "you can take Scott and Matthias with you."

"Why Matthias?" asked Katherine.

"Because," said Mortimer, "he is a helpful young man, and because he's always wanted to see the world outside the Abbey."

"Okay," said Katherine, "I guess we'll get ready to go."

The girls went back to their rooms and changed into clothes more suitable for travel.

*   *   *

Some time later, Isis, Katherine, Scott and Matthias made their way down the road in a cart the Abbey used to bring supplies from town. Isis leaned her head on Scott's shoulder as he held the reins of the roan horse that pulled the cart down the road. Katherine sat in the bed of the cart with Matthias. It was a beautiful day for traveling, the sun shone warmly in the sky and there was a pleasant breeze blowing over the pine trees on either side of the road. The road took them out of the forest and into some grassy hills. As the cart reached the top of the first hill they got their first glimpse of the town.

Mortimer's description of the town as "a very rough place" proved to be apt. It was little more than a cluster of ramshackle buildings with the road running right through the center of it. The cart made its way down the hill and into town. Grim looking townsfolk watched as these strangers in the cart went past them.

"Why are they staring at us?" asked Matthias softly.

"They're trying to see if we're dangerous," said Scott.

"Oh," said Matthias, "okay."

Apparently the townsfolk saw no danger in four teenagers riding in a horse cart. They made their way deeper into town and passed by a seedy looking tavern. If the town was a rough place, than this was a truly wretched hive of scum and villainy. A man dressed in filthy rags stumbled out the door just as the travelers went by. He looked up at them, his eyes red and blurred by drink, he took a few steps toward Isis. He grabbed her roughly by the skirt and tried to pull her off the cart. She let out a shriek and Scott was on the man in flash. He grabbed the drunkard by the collar and hurled him into a nearby water trough. He climbed out of the trough, then rolled over and slumped unconscious. Matthias looked back at the man lying on the ground and then looked at Scott; he was driving the cart farther on its way as if nothing had happened. Matthias suddenly understood one of the reasons why Scott's friends looked up to him; besides the fact he was several inches taller than them. He was a very strong man who was more than capable of keeping them out of trouble.

* * *

Scott pulled the cart in front of a shop and helped Isis and Katherine get off. He followed the girls into the shop and ordered Matthias to watch the cart. The young monk sat on the seat and looked around at the town. It didn't seem so bad. The townspeople were all going about their business, the butcher was preparing a side of beef in his shop, the shopkeepers had set up their wares, and a traveling story teller gathered the children around him and regaled them with local legends. Eventually he started feeling the boredom that comes from waiting by yourself for a long period.

"Hello, are you new around here?" said a silky feminine voice. Matthias turned to see who had spoken; behind him was a beautiful young woman in a revealing red outfit.

"Would you like me to show you around?" she asked in honeyed tones. She fluttered her eyelashes playfully. Matthias sat back and blinked, unsure how to react; fortunately Scott exited the shop at that moment.

"Excuse me," he said to the young woman. She turned around to face him; he was standing in the doorway with his feet squarely planted and his arms across his chest.

"Oh my," she said, clearly impressed by his tall stature and thick muscles that bulged under his tunic.

"Back off hussy," said a very peeved looking Isis also walking out of the shop. The young woman took one look at Isis' expression and made a hasty retreat. Matthias was a bit confused by this occurrence.

"What was that about?" he asked.

Scott snorted and gave that funny half-smile of his,

"I'll tell you when you're older," was all he said on the subject.

* * *

As Scott drove the cart back to the Abbey, Matthias looked at what the girls had purchased in the shop. It was mostly essentials: some basic supplies, a few sets of clothing, nothing unusual. What was unusual was the weapons. Katherine had bought herself a long, elegant rapier while Isis had purchased a pair of daggers. Also unusual was what Scott had purchased. He had bought milk, cream, sugar, mint extract, chocolate and several large blocks of ice packed in sawdust and wrapped in burlap. Matthias spent the whole trip wondering what Scott could make with those ingredients. All that thinking made him hungry so he reached for a bar of chocolate. Scott snapped his hand with the reins. Matthias rubbed the sore spot on his hand and decided to enjoy the scenery of a summer day.

* * *

By the time they got back to the Abbey dinnertime was fast approaching. Scott gathered his ingredients and disappeared into the kitchen.

"What is he going to make with all that?" asked Matthias.

"We'll have to wait and see," replied Katherine.

Before dinner was served, all the residents and guests of the Abbey gathered in the Great Hall, Abbot Mortimer said the blessing and the meal was served. There were three courses: first was a fresh salad with a light dressing, then came roast duck alá orange.

"I don't think there has ever been a meal this large ever served at the Abbey before," said Mortimer. There were hearty agreements all around, and much slackening of belts as well.

"Just a moment Mortimer," said Scott from the kitchen door, "there's one more dish to be served."

"And what might that be?" some one asked.

"Hugo and I prepared a special dessert for everyone," answered Scott.

He returned to the kitchen and came back out with bowls, spoons and a large wooden barrel. Hugo reached into the barrel with a deeply rounded scoop and deposited two servings into a bowl and presented it to the Abbot. Mortimer took a spoon and tasted this dessert. All present waited with anticipation as Mortimer carefully sampled the dish in front of him.

"Delicious," pronounced the Abbot, "What is this?" he asked.

"It's ice cream," said Scott, "mint chocolate chip."

A cheer resounded from the area were Scott's friends were seated. Scott, Hugo and the kitchen staff served dessert and apart from a few cases of brain freeze it was enjoyed by all.

CHAPTER THREE:
A Stellar Discovery

As the days went by Scott's condition improved quite a bit. He needed to use the walking stick less and less. The meals from the kitchens kept getting better as he and Hugo created new and better culinary masterpieces for everyone. But most importantly, William finished the calculations that covered the walls of his room.

"It wasn't easy," William was saying, "to determine this world's spatial position. I had to factor in stellar parallax, spatial coordinates, stellar drift…"

"We get it, it's hard!" interrupted Jon, "now get on with it!"

William rolled his eyes and shook his head slightly.

"I just wanted you guys to know how complicated it was," he said calmly.

"As I was saying," he went on, "after factoring in everything I thought was relevant I was able to determine how far away Midaria is from Earth."

"And how far is that?" asked Loki.

"As near as I can figure," said William, "approximately fifteen hundred and twenty five point one four light-years from Earth."

"Fifteen hundred light-years!" said Loki; understandably he was having trouble comprehending the distance.

"Just about," said William, "I might be wrong though, it's only a rough estimate."

William's friends sat back and spent two whole minutes staring in disbelief. This was understandably shocking, the distance was huge. The nearest star to the Solar system was four light-years away, compared to that fifteen hundred was almost beyond comprehension.

*   *   *

For several days after William's discovery, the group didn't spend much time socializing; mostly they sat in silence while the reality of their situation set in. The end of this spell came in the form of a familiar face, David had returned to the Abbey.

"Hello youngin's," he greeted them cheerily, "I hope ye didn't get into too much trouble while I was gone."

"Well," said Loki, "we did have to take care of some thief that was sneaking around."

David laughed, "Mustn't have been a very good thief if *you* could catch him," he said. Even Scott laughed at that one.

David had brought some things with him from his trip: food, water and other supplies for several days of hard travel. He also brought news from the outside to the Abbey. Apparently, the group's activities at the castle had sparked civil unrest throughout the kingdom. The castle guards were everywhere, searching for the "assassins" who killed the king.

"It was just a misunderstanding," said William, "we weren't trying to hurt anyone; we were just trying to get the book back."

"I seriously doubt they'd see it that way youngin'," said David, "the 'royal guards' are little more than violent thugs with government paychecks."

*   *   *

The eve of David's arrival ended with a delicious meal of venison and a well needed rest before the travelers set out the next day. That morning, Mortimer told Scott some good news--his three weeks were up, and the bandages could come off.

"About time," said Scott.

"Here," said Mortimer, "something for your eye." He handed Scott an eye patch made of black cloth. After unwrapping the bandages Scott slipped the patch over his head laying the string across his face at an angle that went under his ear and around the back of his head.

"Well," asked Scott, "How does it look?"

"Looks good on you," said Mortimer, "Safe journey." He turned and left the room.

Scott packed up his belongings, put on his cloak and hood, buckled his sword over his shoulders and picked up his walking stick. He headed out to the Great Hall where his friends and David were getting ready to go.

"Whoa," said Jon when he looked at Scott's face, "nice looking eye patch."

"Thanks," said Scott.

Jon stood on Scott's right and waved his hand, "Are you sure you'll be able to see?" he asked.

Scott gripped Jon's wrist and squeezed, hard. Jon winced in pain.

"I think I'll be able to see just fine," he said.

David began taking some things out of his pack,

"I got you youngin's some new gear." He told them.

He began passing out the items from his pack: mostly it was essential items like canteens, matches, first-aid kits and other such items that made long distance travel easier. There were not-so-essential items as well: a pair of leather gauntlets with steel plates protecting the forearms, the back of the hands and the knuckles for Scott and a new set of lock picks for Loki.

Katherine suddenly noticed that someone was missing

"Where's William?" she asked.

David knew the answer, "I brought him some decent travelin' clothes," he said, "He's probably just getting out of that ridiculous costume of his."

"That's right," said William as he entered the room. He had indeed shed the ridiculous costume he had worn since arriving on Midaria. He was now dressed in a simple gray tunic, black pants, comfortable looking leather boots and a gray hood and cloak.

Loki gave William's new ensemble a sideways look, "I don't know, Will," he said. "I kind of liked your old outfit. It made you look funnier." Isis hit him.

"Come on youngin's," said David, "get your stuff together and let's go."

"Wait just a moment," said a voice. Mortimer and Matthias walked into the room. They were dressed for travel; Mortimer was outfitted in a green and grey knit sweater, brown trousers, a well-worn pair of boots and a rust-colored cloak. Matthias was dressed in a linen tunic, brown pants, sturdy but oversized leather boots and a brown hood and cloak that were much too long.

"What's this?" asked David.

"Oh come now old friend," said Mortimer, "you didn't honestly expect me to let you have all the fun, did you?"

David chuckled. "I knew you'd want to come along Morty," he said.

"Yes," said Mortimer, "besides, if Scott is any indication, you're going to need good healers, and Matthias and I are the best."

"I suppose that's a good assessment," said Katherine.

"Besides," said Mortimer, "you need someone who won't get lost, David has a tendency to wander."

Everybody laughed as they headed out of the Abbey and down the road towards David's "ship"

*   *   *

Meanwhile, Jessia, James and Krant were on their way out of town after robbing the mayor. They weren't alone however. Several town guards had spotted them when James led them out of all things, the front door.

"Run for it," shouted Krant as the guards pursed them through a narrow alley.

Jessia turned around, dropped her sack of loot and drew her sword. The guards halted and raised their own weapons. The fight was two against one; you really had to feel sorry for the guards. Jessia easily disarmed the guards then slammed one into the wall and dropped the other with a swift blow to the head with her sword's pommel. She sheathed her sword, picked up her sack and continued on her way,

"Let's go," she said calmly. James and Krant exchanged nervous glances and followed her, each making mental notes to not make her angry.

EPISODE III
A SHIP OF THE SKY

CHAPTER ONE:
The Pursuit

The morning after they left the Abbey, the travelers woke up to a delicious breakfast, presumably cooked by Scott but he was nowhere to be seen.

"Where did Scott go?" Matthias asked between mouthfuls.

"I don't know," said David, "he made breakfast and went off into the woods somewhere."

"Hmm," said Mortimer, "that's rather strange."

"Scott is rather strange sometimes Father Abbot," said Matthias.

Mortimer laughed,

"What's so funny Father Abbot?" asked Matthias

"You *can* address me by my name Matthias," said Mortimer, "we're not in the Abbey anymore."

"Okay," said Matthias, "Mortimer."

"There," said the old healer with an encouraging smile, "that wasn't so hard was it."

Ssshhh-thunk, a crossbow quarrel thudded into the tree branch several inches above Mortimer's head.

"Don't move," commanded a voice, it belonged to a skinny young man about the same age as Loki, and he had dark hair that hung down to his shoulders and hazel colored eyes. He held a small crossbow in his nervously shaking hand.

"Hand over all your valuables," ordered a cat-like man with scruffy iron colored hair and beard. Jon and Loki recognized him as the thief from the Abbey.

Mortimer stood up from where he was, he towered over both thieves like an angry bear,

"I don't think we'll be doing that," he said reaching a hand under his cloak.

"Don't even try it old man," said a beautiful woman with flaming red hair and jade green eyes. She held a sword to Mortimer's chest. Mortimer just scowled and was about to push her aside when a loud *crack* split the air, everyone turned to see where it came from.

Scott had returned from his sojourn in the woods and when seeing his friends in danger snapped a branch off of a nearby tree. The branch was as thick as his forearm and made for an excellent cudgel.

"I got him," said Krant as he drew his dagger and charged at the branch wielding muscleman who had interrupted their robbery. A blow to the stomach sent him sprawling. James dropped his crossbow, gave a rather effeminate scream and ran face first into a tree. Jessia was unimpressed,

"You won't best me as easily as you did my companions," she said taking up a fighting stance.

Scott didn't say a word; he just brandished his cudgel and prepared to fight. Jessia moved to his right side and swung at his head. He ducked the swinging blade and took a swing at his opponent's midsection. She nimbly dodged the blow and swung at him with all she had. *Chunkk*, the blade bit deeply into the branch when Scott raised it in defense, his opponent certainly looked surprised. She had apparently thought he wouldn't be able to see her on that side because of the patch over his eye. What she didn't know was that he could hear her attacks coming due to the whistling of her sword blade through the air.

The two warriors played a brief game of tug of war as Jessia tried to pull her sword out of the branch and Scott tried to wrest the blade from her hands. Suddenly Scott let go and she fell to the ground. She stood back up and took a swing at a tree that happened to be within arms reach. The branch split like a piece of firewood,

"Ha!" exclaimed Jessia, "now you don't have a weapon."

Scott just smiled that wry half smile of his and chuckled softly,

"I wouldn't be too sure of that," he said as he brought his sword out from under his cloak and buckled it on over his shoulder. As he drew the huge blade from its scabbard, Jessia's eyes nearly bugged out of her skull in surprise, the immense blade was nearly as long as she was tall. Scott swung the sword playfully with his hand, the razor keen edges made a loud thrumming noise as the blade moved through the air. Jessia gulped and raised her sword in defense. Scott spun around with lightning speed and struck her in the head with the cross-guard of his sword. Her eyes rolled back in their sockets and she dropped like a brick.

"Way too easy," said Scott as he sheathed his sword. He walked over to his friend's camp and sat down like nothing had happened.

"Hey look Jon," said Loki as he stood over the unconscious Krant, "it's our friend from the Abbey."

"Yep," agreed Jon, "it sure is."

"You think maybe he followed us from the Abbey?" asked Loki.

"I doubt it," said David, who happened to over hear them, "I heard that someone robbed the mayor of the town near the Abbey. The description fits these three here."

Jon and Loki dragged the unconscious bandits into the woods and leaned them up against a tree. Scott cleaned his cooking utensils and packed them away.

"Where are we going?" asked Isis.

"Off the island," said David.

"How?" asked Matthias, "there aren't any ships on Ikaros."

"I know of one," said David, "It belongs to an old friend of Morty and me."

"Really," said Mortimer, "I didn't expect him to stay in one place for so long."

"He didn't," said David, "he happened to be here when I went looking for him."

Mortimer gave him a funny look, "You have a knack for that," he told his friend.

"So where is this ship?" asked Jon.

"That way," said David pointing due west, "if we leave now it's only a day and a half trip."

"Well then," said Mortimer, "let's go. I could use a change of scenery after all these years."

"Why?" asked Matthias, "the island is beautiful."

"That may be true," said Mortimer, "but there's a whole big world out there Matthias. I've lived on Ikaros for fourteen years and seen every inch of it. I want you to experience what life has to offer and you can't have that here on this little island."

"Okay," said Matthias, "let's go." He picked up his pack and his favorite ash staff and headed off to the west. Mortimer looked after him and chuckled,

"Ah, to be young again," he said, "he's a lot like I was at his age. Energetic and impatient."

"I remember," said David. The grizzled Wanderer led the way to catch up with Matthias.

*   *   *

About an hour after the travelers headed off, the three thieves started coming around. James woke up first; he had several sore spots on his face from running into the tree. Krant stirred, then sat up with a groan,

"Ohhh, I feel like a mountain dropped on me," he said.

"I believe you," said James, "did you see the size of that guy."

"Yeah," said Krant as he tried to stand.

James the noticed Jessia's prone form leaning against the tree. Krant noticed as well,

"He beat Jessia," he said in disbelief, "that ain't good."

They roused her awake, she was in a fouler mood than usual.

"That snotty kid beat me," she growled, "I'll get him next time."

"Jessia, he's twice your size," said James, "how do you expect to beat him."

"Simple," said the swordswoman, "I'll cheat."

"Hey," said Krant, "our loot's still here. Let's go."

The thieves grabbed their sacks and headed off to the west. Unaware that they were not only following the travelers, but being followed as well.

*   *   *

David led the travelers across a grassy clearing. Mortimer and Matthias were three steps behind followed by Scott and Isis then William, Katherine, Jon and Loki.

"Mortimer," said Matthias, "How did you meet David?" he asked.

"When David and I first met," began Mortimer, "I was no more than your age. I was a young recruit in the Veridean Royal Guard, he was my commanding officer."

"David is older than you!" Matthias said incredulously.

"I know," said Mortimer, "he certainly doesn't look it does he. In fact, from the first day I met him he hasn't aged at all."

"How is that possible?" asked Isis.

"I don't know," said Mortimer, "there are many things about David that are a mystery."

"Hey!" said David, "Quiet down back there youngin's."

"Why does he call us that?" asked Matthias.

Mortimer chuckled, "he calls anyone younger than himself that," he said, "he called me that for twenty-eight years."

"Quiet!" commanded David.

"What's his problem," said Jon.

"I think someone's following us," said David.

"How do you figure that?" asked Loki.

"Run for it!" shouted a voice. Jessia, James and Krant ran by them as fast as they could.

"That's a pretty good indication," said David calmly.

There was a soft hissing noise and an arrow landed point first into the soil beside Jon.

"If anyone needs me," he said, "I'll be following them." He started to run after the thieves.

"You there, Halt!" commanded a voice. The group turned around to see Malagent leading a contingent of guards towards them.

"Well, well," said the rodent like man when he saw their faces, "it appears we've found our fugitives."

"Give it up will you," said an exasperated David, "we both know you were trying to kill the king long before we got to him."

"That may be true," said Malagent, "but *you* were the ones to kill the king, and for that you are to be arrested, tried and executed."

Mortimer gave David a funny look, "that has a familiar ring to it doesn't it," he told his old friend.

David returned the glance, "I do believe it does old friend," he said to Mortimer.

Mortimer looked over Malagent and the guards for a moment then looked at David again,

"What do you think?" he asked, "The usual?"

David also assessed the guards before turning to Mortimer again,

"The usual," he pronounced. The two veterans nodded and drew out large handguns from somewhere on their persons. David had the same futuristic looking semi-automatic while Mortimer had a seven shot revolver. Malagent's eyes widened in surprise,

"Ohh," he said quickly stepping behind his troops, "Gentlemen, if you would be so kind as to relieve them of their weapons." He clapped his hands and the guards began walking toward the travelers.

David looked at Mortimer, "Why is it that the bad guy always sends his lackeys to do the work?" he asked.

"I have no idea," said Mortimer, "rather cowardly I should say." The old healer pulled back the hammer of his revolver and fired at the ground in front of a guard's feet. Most of the armored men jumped back at the shot. One of them however drew his sword and charged forward. David took aim and squeezed off a round from his own sidearm. There was a flash of azure light and a high-pitched whine sound and the guard flew backward into the grass,

"Care to join him?" David asked the other guards. Before they could do anything however, Malagent spoke up,

"Now!" shouted the weasel-like Chief Justiciary, several platoons of guards charged out of the woods behind him.

"That could be a problem," said David, "run for it youngin's!"

The group headed for the woods with abandon. David and Mortimer would occasionally turn to fire; several of the guards were hit. Eventually they lost their pursuers and sat down to catch their breath by an elm tree overlooking a stream. By coincidence Jessia, James and Krant were at the same place.

"Wow," said James, "you guys were incredible."

"It was nothing," said David as he and Mortimer reloaded their weapons, "Morty and me used to do that sort of thing all the time."

"Yes," said Mortimer as he spun the cylinder of his revolver, "we were once the personal guardians of the king of Veridea."

"Were you in the palace during Dragon Eye's coup?" asked Krant.

"What interest is it of yours?" asked David, as if to emphasize his point he closed the slide of his semi-automatic with a loud click.

"I just thought you might know where the royal family escaped to," said the cat-like thief, "there are a lot of people who think it's about time they fought back."

"Sadly," said Mortimer, "we don't know where they went. But if you want someone to fight back, then I don't think you'll have to wait much longer." He cast a brief glance to where Scott was busy making lunch.

"So," said Jon, "where do we head off to next?" he asked.

"We can follow the river this stream connects to," said David, "it'll take us all the way down to where we're going."

Scott finished making lunch and wandered off into the woods.

"Where's he going?" asked James.

"Scott likes to spend sometime by himself," said Katherine, "it helps him stay calm while having to deal with Hekyll and Jekyll over there." She nodded her head towards Jon and Loki. James laughed, then remembered something important,

"Sorry about trying to rob you," he told her, "No hard feelings?"

"Hmmph," said Jessia.

"Come on Jess," said James, "you saw what they did to those guards."

Jessia made a growling noise, "All right," she said, "sorry."

*   *   *

After walking some distance into the woods Scott came across a small clearing with an ancient willow tree standing in the middle of it like a lonely giant. Breathing a sigh of content, he drew his sword from the scabbard on his back and thrust it point first into the mossy soil. He threw back his hood and sat cross-legged on the ground. He closed his eyes and took a few deep breaths to gather his thoughts.

He thought about quite a few things, like how he and his friends had come to this new world and where they would go from this island. He thought about this guy David, who was he? Why was he interested in helping them? He also thought about Isaac, the young man who looked almost exactly like him. How was that possible? He decided to put these questions aside for later and allowed himself to relax. His hand went to the eye patch he no wore, I wonder what my friends will think, he thought, I know Isis will think it makes me look distinctive.

He closed his eyes and listened to the sounds of the forest. He could hear the river, his friends and the thieves talking amongst themselves, the sounds of wildlife moving through the trees. Then he heard a new sound, footsteps coming up behind him, he didn't recognize them. They were tired, world weary but the quick, undeviating pace indicated someone with iron determination. While pondering why this person would be following him he heard another sound, the steely rasp of a sword being drawn from its scabbard. This immediately told him who was approaching from behind.

He counted off the steps until the person was right behind him and heard the tell-tale whistle of a sword strike. In one fluid motion, he whirled around, grabbed up his sword and blocked the attack. He opened his eyes and was not at all surprised to find that the person who had followed him was Isaac. The black-cloaked young man had a patch over his left eye just like the one across his own right eye. The look-alike regarded him with that calm blue grey eye that was the same as his,

"Not bad," said Isaac, "I suppose I should have expected you'd hear me coming."

"So," said Scott, "I suppose you're here to finish our fight from the castle."

"Yes I am," said Isaac, "so I suppose we should get on with it."

"Indeed we should," said Scott. The two warriors crossed swords and began to finish their duel.

*   *   *

Scott's friends were enjoying their lunch when they suddenly heard a metallic ringing sound, the sounds of a fierce sword fight.

"Please don't tell me that's what I think it is," said Jon.

"It sounds like someone's having a sword fight," said James.

"I said *don't* tell me,"

"Come on youngin's," said David, "we might be able to stop it."

They set down their meal, grabbed their weapons and headed towards the sound.

*   *   *

The oddly musical ring of steel on steel filled the air as Scott and Isaac dueled across the clearing.

"You're quite the swordsman," said Isaac as he parried an overhand slash from Scott.

"You're not so bad yourself," returned Scott as he neatly deflected a thrust from Isaac.

The two fenced back and forth across the grass, both were more or less evenly matched. While Scott had more muscle than Isaac, the look-alike had the speed to intercept everything Scott threw at him. In fact he even seemed to enjoy it, Scott felt the same. When Scott's friends arrived on the scene they were surprised as Scott was to see Isaac.

"Oh great," said Loki exasperatedly, "not him again!"

The three thieves were rather surprised by the appearance of the two swordfighters,

"They look almost exactly alike!" said James.

"Yes," said David casting a strange glance at Mortimer, "it's almost like looking at a mirror."

"Indeed it is," said Mortimer with a strange smile, "interesting isn't it."

Scott and Isaac locked their swords together, their faces no longer bearing the expressions of mortal enemies; instead they looked like old friends.

"You're making this quite a challenge," said Scott with a friendly smile, "Keep it up."

Isaac gave an identical grin to Scott's, "Certainly," he said politely. They pushed away from each other and resumed their duel. They matched each other blow for blow, their blades ringing a merry symphony across the clearing.

"Wow," said Jessia as she watched the two of them, "they're good."

"We know," said Jon, "we watched them duel back at the castle."

Scott and Isaac continued to duel, neither showing any signs of tiring. Jon looked at them for a few minutes then turned around,

"I'm going back to camp," he said, "I think there going to be at it for a while."

Jon's assessment proved to be quite accurate, it was sunset by the time Scott and Isaac finally tired each other out. They were laughing as they came back to camp.

"I can't believe I was actually trying to kill you over a book," said Isaac, "how stupid is that."

"You two seem to be getting along well," Katherine told them.

Scott and Isaac took long drinks from canteens then dumped the rest over their heads.

"Well," said Isaac, "about two minutes into the fight, we started enjoying it. I guess it just went from there."

"Stranger things have happened," said David with a shrug. He and Mortimer had strange looks in their eyes.

Scott prepared dinner while David, Jon and Krant went to find firewood. Afterwards the travelers, the thieves and Isaac all sat around the campfire and talked for a bit. Isaac looked over at David and Mortimer,

"I heard gunfire earlier," he said, "was that you?"

"Yes," said Mortimer, "that was us."

"I don't know why we had to run," said Isis, "I could have stopped them with this." She waved her hand and a shimmering field of energy appeared between a pair of trees.

"Whoa!" said Krant shaking his head slightly, "what was that?"

"Sorcery," said Isaac.

"How do you know that?" asked James.

Isaac clenched his fist then slowly opened his hand, small sparks of energy crackled around and between his fingers. James stared wide eyed, Isaac only smiled,

"Does that answer your question," he said.

"That's cool," said William.

"It is, isn't it," said Isaac, "but also very dangerous."

"What do you mean?"

"When Alaraune Dragon Eye staged his coup in Veridea, he outlawed sorcery under pain of death."

"That's inhuman," said Katherine.

"Clearly you've never met the man," said Mortimer.

"Aye," said David, "he sold his own soul for power."

Isaac decided to change the subject, "Where are you going from here?"

"We're heading to the coast," David told him, "there's a ship waiting for us."

"Mind if I come along?" asked Isaac.

David and Mortimer looked at each other and smiled,

"That would be fine," said David.

"Okay then," said Isaac, he yawned loudly, "guess I'll turn in for the night."

He walked over to where he had laid out his bed roll and went to sleep.

"All right youngin's" said David, "off to bed with ye."

"David and I will take the first watch," said Mortimer.

There were grumbles all around as the travelers got up from around the warm fire and went over to their bed rolls.

"You too," David told the thieves, "we've got a long day tomorrow."

The thieves complied, if nothing else out of self-preservation, they certainly didn't want to mess with a pair of armed soldiers.

* * *

The next morning after breakfast, they followed the river. David led them down a path that went along the riverbank.

"Where are we going?" asked Jon, "all I keeping seeing is forest."

"You'll find out shortly youngin'," said David, "We're almost there."

David was right; as soon as they went around the next bend of the river they spotted their destination. A large aircraft hanger overlooking a cliff.

"What kind of ship would need a building like that?" asked Matthias.

"You'll find out soon enough youngin'" said David. The grizzled Wanderer led them towards the building.

"Come on," he said, "that's where our ride is."

CHAPTER TWO:
The Griffin

"What kind of ship would need a building like this?" asked Matthias for the second time.

"You'll see," said Mortimer, "just as soon as they let us in."

The travelers were quite impressed by the sheer size of the structure. It looked just like any aircraft hanger except for one detail.

"Where are the doors?" asked William.

"What do you mean by that youngin'?" asked David.

"It is an airplane hanger isn't it," said William, "there should be big sliding doors on the front."

"This hanger isn't for a plane William," said Mortimer.

"Then what is it for?" asked Katherine.

"Wait and see," said the old healer.

There was a wooden door in the front wall. David walked up to it and knocked three times.

"What is it?" asked a voice from within,

"It's us Gene," said Mortimer, "we're told you'd get us off the island."

The door opened and out stepped a tall broad-shouldered man in a burgundy sweater and black trousers. He had close cropped white hair and beard with friendly brown eyes. He took a few pulls from a wooden pipe and grinned.

"Mortimer, David," he said, "good to see you."

"Hello Gene," said David, "I was hoping you'd still be here."

Mortimer turned to the travelers and thieves,

"This is our good friend Captain Gene Swift," he said, "captain of the airship *Griffin*."

"Airship!" said William.

"That's right," said Capt. Swift, "an airship. And one of the finest ever built if I do say so myself."

Matthias raised his hand,

"What's an airship?" he asked.

Captain Swift laughed, "Come on in," he said, "I'll show you."

* * *

The airship *Griffin* was a majestic vehicle. Its gleaming pearlescent finish reflected rainbow hues in the bright electric lights of the hanger. It had a vaguely boat shaped hull, with metal rings surfaced with crystal around the inside along the sides and huge three propeller rotors on the stern.

"The *Griffin* was built as a luxury transport," Capt. Swift told his guests, "in fact; she belonged to the Veridean royal family until the coup. She's been to nearly every port in the world."

"Wow," was all Matthias could say.

"What are those rings at the bow and stern for?" asked William.

"Ah," said the Captain, "those rings are what make the ship fly. When energy is diverted into the crystals they create a negative gravity field."

"Whoa," said William, "that's cool."

"Very cool," agreed Capt. Swift.

"Gene," said Mortimer, "while I know full well you enjoy giving tours of your ship, we really do need to get going."

"Aye," said David, "We've got--"

The door to the hanger burst open and several armed guards entered, followed by Malagent,

"Stay where you are!" the weasel-like man ordered.

"Them," finished David.

Captain Swift snapped his fingers twice and looked to his crew,

"Gents," he said, "would you care to show these men how we treat unwanted guests."

Several crewmen jumped to the crates stacked around the hanger and opened them. These crates contained weapons: rifles, submachine guns and explosives, enough to fight a small war. Malagent and his guards suddenly found themselves facing dozens of loaded guns.

"How dare you," growled Malagent, "I am a servant of the king of Ikaros."

"Well, well," said Capt. Swift, "If it isn't the little traitor Malagent." The captain drew a nickel-plated handgun from the holster on his belt.

"I see only one traitor here, Royalist," said Malagent.

Captain Swift smiled, "I prefer to think of myself as a patriot," he told Malagent.

"Patriot or not," said Malagent, "You're still rebel scum."

David drew his own hand gun,

"Go back to your master, lapdog," he said fiercely, "and tell him that his day is coming."

Malagent glared at David,

"Very well," he said, "but you haven't seen the last of me. The next time we meet will be your last." He twisted the gem of the ring on his right hand, a blood red ruby set in a dragon's claw. In a flash of light and a small explosion, Malagent disappeared, leaving his guards to face the crew of the *Griffin*.

"Looks like your boss saved his own skin," Captain Swift told the guards, "What are you going to do?"

The guards threw down their weapons and reached for the ceiling. Captain Swift and his men put their weapons down.

"Get out of here," he told the guards, "and don't come back to this hanger."

The frightened guards nodded, picked up their arms and fled.

"Well," said the Captain, "now that that's over with, shall we get under way?" he asked the travelers.

"By all means," said David, "let's go youngin's."

They followed the Captain up a boarding ramp into the ship. Capt. Swift pressed a button on the ship's intercom,

"This is the Captain," he said into the speaker, "all hands prepare for launch."

A buzzer sounded twice and the crew of the *Griffin* went to work fulfilling the Captain's orders. Captain Swift turned to his passengers,

"Would you care to watch from the bridge?" he asked. He got positive answers all around,

"Follow me please," he told them. He led them upstairs five decks to the bridge of the airship. The room was full of navigational displays and controls; it looked very much like the bridge of a World War Two aircraft carrier. There was a comfortable looking chair located more or less in the center; it was occupied by a tall young man in a cowboy hat.

"Cid!" yelled the Captain, the young man shot up out of the chair immediately.

"Yes sir?" he asked in a thick west Texas drawl.

"Don't sit in my chair," said the Captain, "Cid my helmsman," he told the travelers, "as you can see he has ambitions of command." He smiled and chuckled slightly.

"Captain," said a crewman, "Engine Room reports generators at one hundred percent."

"Very good," said the Captain, "commence launch."

The bridge crew worked at their stations, a subtle vibration could be felt

79

through the deck. Overhead, the roof of the hanger began to slide open to allow the ship to take off.

"Activate floatation generators," ordered the Captain. A crewman pressed several switches at his station. Outside, the crystal lining of the generator rings began to shine with warm light. The ship began to rise slightly.

"Take us up," said Capt. Swift. Cid pushed a throttle like control at his station, the ship gained altitude even faster, as soon as it cleared the hanger the doors began to close. Captain Swift crossed over to his chair and sat down,

"Come right to course zero-four-five," he said, "altitude twenty five hundred feet, speed twenty six knots."

Cid adjusted a knob at his station then spun the steering wheel. The *Griffin* began turning around one hundred thirty five degrees to point due northeast. The propellers at the stern began to spin, a rhythmic thrumming sounded from deep within the ship. As soon as the ship began to move forward, Cid tilted the wheel back and the ship rose into a gradual climb. Soon the beautiful ship was cruising gracefully among the clouds.

"Altitude twenty five hundred feet, speed twenty six knots, heading zero-four-five degrees," reported Cid. The Captain nodded.

"Navigator," he said.

"Yes sir," came the reply in a clipped British accent.

"Richard," said the Captain, "lay in a course to Port Marraka."

"Aye sir," said the Navigator. He twisted several knobs at his station and flipped a switch. There was a map of the world on the wall above his station. There were several lights activated on it, a blue one to mark the position of the *Griffin*, a gold one marked the destination and several red lights indicated the course.

"Course laid in," reported Richard, "estimated time to destination, two days."

"Very good," said the Captain he turned to his passengers, "Now, please allow me to show you around."

*   *   *

The interior of the *Griffin* was tastefully decorated and very comfortable. The walls were covered with dark wood paneling and the floors with thick, soft carpet. Captain Swift gave his guests a full tour of the ship, starting with the Engine Room.

"Our Chief Engineer prides himself on being able to fix anything," he was telling them, "we like to call him 'the miracle worker'." He led them down a flight of stairs to the bottom level of the Engine Room where a white-haired, barrel-bodied man in a black vest over a white sweater and black trousers was giving orders in a thick Scottish brogue. Captain Swift introduced his "miracle worker."

"This is Scott Montgomery," he said, "the best Engineer anywhere."

"Aye," said the Engineer, "but most people call me Monty. Come on, ah'll show ye 'round." Captain Swift stepped back and let Monty show the travelers around his domain.

"How de ye like mah engine room?" asked Monty.

"It's very clean," said James.

"Thank ye laddie," said Monty, "I like tae keep mah engines clean, they work better that way."

He showed them the massive generators that powered the whole ship and explained how they worked,

"Th' whole system works off sun crystals," he told them, "th' crystals contain and store magical energy. When ye give 'em a jolt, they release that energy which we can send tae th' flotation generators or tae th' turbines."

"And the turbines turn the propellers and power the ship," said William.

"Aye," said Monty stroking his black handlebar mustache, "yer pretty smart fer a wee one." Isis giggled at that, William just blinked.

"Thanks," he said, "I think."

Captain Swift came back to join them,

"Well I see Monty's all done with his portion of the tour," he said, "if you'll follow me I'll show you the rest of the ship." He led them forward through the cargo hold then up two levels to the stateroom deck.

"These are where you'll be staying during the voyage," said the Captain, "I'm sure they'll be to your liking." He took them up to the lounge deck next, this level had the dining room, a small theatre, a couple of well appointed sitting rooms and had an exterior deck running all the way around outside. Also on this deck was a very large library. Upon entering this room, Scott and Isaac left the group, picked a couple of books off the shelves and sat down in armchairs.

"Looks like they've made themselves at home," said Katherine.

Captain Swift laughed, "So it would seem," he said, "that's it for the tour. You can explore the ship on your own if you like or go back to your staterooms." He headed back up to the bridge. The travelers went their own ways around the ship, the three thieves went to their staterooms and hid there, Jon, Loki and the girls got a card game going and William and Matthias decided to give themselves more detailed tours of the ship.

*   *   *

Back in the Library, Scott and Isaac had done some redecorating. They had moved the chairs and tables around to what they thought were a more comfortable layout. Scott had just sat down in his chair by the window when David came in the room.

"Hello youngin's," he said cheerily, "I see you've found the library. Didn't have trouble finding something to read I hope."

"No we didn't," said Isaac, "somehow we knew where all the books were on the shelves."

"Really," said David, "that's interesting." The Wanderer walked over and sat down in a chair near Scott's.

"That's a rather nice sword you've got there youngin'," he said looking at the huge blade leaning up against the wall.

"Yes," said Scott, "it is."

David stood up and picked up the heavy sword and drew it from its scabbard, he hefted it like it weighed nothing at all.

"Tis a beautiful blade," he said admiringly, "at one time it might have belonged to a king." He had a sly half smile as he said that. David sheathed the sword and put it back,

"I'll see you youngin's later," he said as he walked out the door leaving Scott and Isaac to their reading.

*   *   *

Matthias was having the time of his life. For most of his life, he had never been outside the Abbey walls and now here he was traveling on an airship. He wandered the halls admiring the view through the windows and the paintings that decorated the walls. This place was beautiful and had a sense of calm and peace that made him feel right at home. Eventually, he found himself in the Library, Isaac had left, but Scott was still there.

"Hello Matthias," said Scott looking up from his book, "what brings you here?"

"I don't know," said Matthias, "I was just wandering around and ended up here."

"This little adventure getting to be a little too much for you," said Scott.

"Yes," said Matthias, "I never dreamed that I'd ever get to do something like this, going out into the world, meeting new friends, traveling on an airship. I never imagined an adventure like this."

"Me either," said Scott.

"What do you mean?" asked Matthias.

"I was transported from a whole other planet remember," said Scott.

"So what do you do about something like this?" asked the young healer.

"I try to keep an open mind, said Scott, "that way I'm ready for the unexpected."

"That sounds like a good idea," said Matthias, "I guess I'll try that."

He left the room and decided to go see what the others were doing. Scott went and got another book.

CHAPTER THREE:
The Brothers Wolf

Isaac sat in his room looking out the window at the ocean. He enjoyed these quiet moments of solitude. They helped him calm down and organize his thoughts. He sat on the bed, legs crossed and eye closed listening to the rhythms of the ship. Despite his awareness of his surroundings, he was startled by the sound of his door opening. The grizzled Wanderer known as David entered the room,

"I thought you'd be in here," he said in that archaic accent of his, "I need ye to come with me youngin',"

"What for?" asked Isaac.

"Just follow me," said the Wanderer.

Isaac got up off the bed and followed David down the hall and up stairs to the lounge deck, then to the Library. David knocked on the door and it opened to reveal Scott, the only person Isaac considered his equal with a sword and rather strangely, a friend.

"Can I help you?" asked Scott in his gruff tone.

"Come with us youngin'," said David, "We have something to discuss."

Scott went back into the room to put his book away,

David led the boys to one of the lounges toward the stern; all of Scott's friends were there. The boorish swordsman Jon; Loki the thief; Isis, whom he supposed was Scott's girlfriend; her brother William, keeper of that special book; the young healer Matthias and the beautiful Katherine. Also in attendance was the ship's Captain and the old healer Mortimer.

"Have a seat," Mortimer told them.

"What's going on?" asked Isaac.

"Well," said David, "if you're going to be travelin' with us Isaac. It's only fair that we all get to know you."

"I suppose," said Isaac, sitting in a big plush armchair, "Where would you like me to start?"

"From the beginning I suppose," said Mortimer, "How about telling us about your family."

Isaac sighed sadly, "I'm an orphan," he said, "I never really had a family."

"That's terrible," said Katherine, "no one to spend good times with or keep you company."

"I don't really mind," said Isaac, "I've lived most of my life on my own."

"Really," said Jon, "how did that come to happen?"

"Well," said Isaac, "when I was a boy I lived with a woodsman and his family. But when my magical abilities began to manifest they kicked me out to keep Dragon Eye's men away."

"That's rather cruel," said William.

"Yes," said Isaac, "but unfortunately it's a fact of life. Alaraune Draconan would never allow anyone with sorcerer's powers to threaten his rule."

"Did you ever try to find your birth parents?" asked Isis.

"No," said Isaac, "I was never even told about them."

"Perhaps we could help with that," said Mortimer.

Isaac cocked an eyebrow quizzically, "What are you talking about?" he asked.

Mortimer smiled slyly, "The three of us knew your parents," he said, "myself, David and Gene."

"You did," said Isaac.

"Aye," said David, "Scott's too."

"How could that be," said Scott, "my parents were from Denver. At least my mother was, I never knew my father."

"Oh, I wouldn't be so sure," said Mortimer, "tell me Scott. Did your mother have a streak of white hair?"

"Yeah," said Scott cocking his eyebrow in the same way as Isaac, "but what does that have to do with anything?"

"Look at Isaac," said the old healer.

Scott looked at the young man who strangely looked just like him. They both had the same aristocratic features and the same calm, blue grey eye, they even wore their eye patches the same way but Isaac had one differing characteristic: a single lock of white hair that stuck up at an odd angle.

"Haven't you wondered how you both look almost exactly alike?" asked Captain Swift.

He had a point. Isaac had indeed wondered how someone he had never met before could look so similar.

"A little," admitted Scott.

"Why are you asking this?" asked Isaac.

"Because," said Captain Swift, "fourteen years ago we were the guardians of the Veridean royal family, the King, the Queen and their twin sons."

"How does this concern us?" asked Scott.

"Because," said Mortimer, "we'd recognize the Wolf brothers no matter how old they get."

That statement sparked something in the minds of Scott and Isaac.

"What do you mean 'Wolf brothers'?" asked Scott, "I'm an only child."

"No you aren't," said David, "you have a twin brother." He looked over at Isaac.

"You're kidding right," said Jon.

"Nope," said Captain Swift.

Scott and Isaac stared at each other, each now seeing truth in their own faces,

"Whoa," they said together.

"Okay," said Jon, "how did that happen?"

Captain Swift told the tale, "During the coup," he began, "the palace was shelled by Alaraune's insurgents. We thought we lost Isaac."

The old Captain walked over, out his hand on Isaac's shoulder and squeezed. He had a very strong grip.

"And now the sons of Veridea are reunited," he said.

"Come on gents," said David to his old comrades, "let's give them some time to talk." He led them from the room to let Scott, Isaac and the rest of the party alone.

"Wow!" said Jon, "this… this is incredible."

"It is certainly an interesting turn of events," agreed Isaac.

"You can say that again," said Scott.

"This is so cool," said Loki, "my best friend is royalty. I'll be able to steal anything and get away with--" Scott and Isaac got up out of their chairs, walked across the room and slapped him on the back of the head before he got any further.

"Does he always think only of himself?" asked Isaac.

"Pretty much," said Scott.

"We can usually keep him in line though," said Katherine.

Isaac looked at his newfound brother and his friends,

"Your little group seems very much like a family," he assessed.

"It does doesn't it," said Katherine, "and it's very easy to tell who the parents are."

"I guess I could get used to being in a family," said Isaac.

"Well," said Scott, "if my brother is going to be part of the 'family', its only fair that we introduce ourselves."

"Okay," said William, "I'll go first." He stood up and shook Isaac's hand,

"I'm William Evans," he said, "And this is my big sister Isis." Isaac bowed his head respectfully towards her,

"My lady," he said.

Katherine stood and offered a handshake,

"I'm Katherine Belmont," she told him. Isaac bowed deeply and kissed her hand,

"Pleased to meet you Lady Katherine," he said politely. Katherine seemed flattered, but Jon tried to make a growling noise in his throat, it came out sounding like a belch.

"That's my brother, Jon," said Katherine, "don't worry, he's harmless."

Jon glared at his sister, Isaac laughed. Loki took Isaac's hand and shook it vigorously,

"I'm Loki Burne," he said, "professional thief."

"I gathered that," said Isaac.

"And my name is Matthias," said the young healer.

"Pleased to meet you Matthias," said Isaac, "and pleased to meet all of you, my brother has very fine friends."

"Now if you'll excuse us," said Scott, "my brother and I have a lot of catching up to do." The two brothers left the room and headed back to the library.

Scott's friends were quite astounded by this new development,

"Wow," said William, "that's not something that happens every day."

"Yeah," said Jon, "I couldn't imagine what I'd feel like if I suddenly found out I had a twin brother."

Katherine shuddered, "Don't even suggest that," she said, "one of you is bad enough."

Loki burst out laughing, Jon hit him.

*   *   *

The Wolf brothers were getting to know one another in the Library. Isaac was especially curious as to what his parents were like,

"You said you never knew our father," he told his brother, "What happened?"

Scott's expression sobered and he sighed sadly, he had never liked discussing this topic,

"He disappeared when I was three," he said, "I never knew what happened to him."

"You never even saw him," said Isaac.

Scott nodded, "Only in an old picture that mother kept on the mantle."

"Could you tell me about her?" Isaac asked, "Our mother I mean."

"What's there to say," said Scott, "she was kind and beautiful and…sad." His expression saddened at the last words, "It was like she always felt sorry for herself."

"What do you mean?" asked his brother.

"Well," said Scott, "I guess she felt sorry for having to leave her home and everything she loved."

"What happened to her?" asked Isaac.

"She died," said Scott sadly.

"That's terrible," said Isaac, "what happened?"

"She was in an accident," said Scott.

"Oh," said Isaac, "I'm sorry." He walked over and gave his brother a sympathetic hug.

"Thanks," said Scott.

The door opened suddenly and Loki Burne swept into the room like a lanky hurricane.

"Hey guys," he said, "how are you getting along?"

"Quite fine," said Isaac.

"No new battle scars?" asked Loki. Isaac laughed.

"Whoa," said Loki, caught a bit off guard, "You actually have a sense of humor, try to warn me next time."

Scott laughed that time.

"Well," said Loki, "I guess I'll leave you two alone." He left the room and it was quiet again. The twins sat reading for a while and listened to the sounds of the ship. Eventually a knock sounded on the door.

"Come in," said Scott.

Mortimer opened the door and entered, the brothers looked up from their books,

"Hello boys," said Mortimer.

"Hello Mortimer," said the twins.

"What brings you here?" asked Scott.

"I wanted to see your sword," said Mortimer.

"My sword," said Scott a tad bit confused.

"Yes," said Mortimer, "your sword. The Sword of Light."

"You're kidding right," said Isaac.

"No I'm not," replied Mortimer.

"Mind telling me what's going on?" asked Scott.

Mortimer took a seat and looked at the two young men.

"The Sword of Light is the treasure of your family," he began, "it was created a thousand years ago by the founder of your family line. He forged together a strange, meteoric metal and a sun crystal to create a blade that would never dull or age and absorb magical energy."

"That explains what happened at the castle," said Scott.

Mortimer nodded in agreement then continued with his history lesson,

"Over the centuries, the blade was passed from father to son each wielder becoming the king of Veridea."

"What would happen if there was more than one son?" asked Isaac.

"The sword would be given to whoever wanted it," answered Mortimer, "After all, not everyone wants to rule a kingdom."

"I can understand why," said Scott, "it takes a lot of responsibility."

"Yes," said Mortimer, "so Scott, are you ready for the job?"

Scott cocked an eyebrow.

"You are the one with the sword," said Mortimer.

"Oh," said Scott, he paused to consider the notion, "Sure, why not."

"That's good to hear," said Mortimer, "I'll go tell that to David." He opened the door and left the twins to their reading.

*   *   *

Up on the bridge, everything was proceeding as normal. Captain Swift sat in his chair with a cup of coffee and enjoyed the view through the windows. It was just another routine run until,

"Conn, Radar," came the announcement from the radar room. Captain Swift thumbed the switch on his intercom mike,

"Conn aye," he said, "go ahead Alex."

"Yes sir," said the radar tech, "large contact approaching directly astern, it seems to be following us."

"Can you identify it?" asked the Captain.

"The radar signature identifies it as a Veridean cruiser."

Captain Swift did a spit take into his coffee mug and swore.

"Sir," called the radioman, "incoming transmission from the cruiser."

"Patch it through," ordered the Captain.

"We meet again Captain Swift," said the irritatingly familiar voice over the radio.

"Malagent," said Captain Swift, "I should have known you'd head back to your boss."

"I haven't yet," said Malagent, "I decided to finish my business with yourself and your crew before I returned to Veridea."

Captain Swift could imagine Malagent sitting confidently on the bridge of the cruiser, barely filling the center seat with his small frame.

"Increase to flank, take evasive action," ordered the Captain. Cid increased speed and began following a zigzag course. The cruiser rapidly fell behind.

"That solves that," said the Captain. It was then that a deep concussive thud sounded directly astern. The *Griffin* shook violently.

"They're firing on us!" said Cid.

The Captain thumbed the intercom switch again,

"All hands man your battle stations," he ordered. A buzzing klaxon sounded and the ship immediately became a hive of frenzied activity as the crew prepared for the ship for a fight. Mortimer, David, the young travelers, and the three thieves arrived on the bridge shortly after.

"What's happening?" they asked.

"We're under attack," said the Captain, "Malagent again."

"He doesn't give up does he," said James.

"Yeah," said the Captain, "but I'm not about to chalk one up to him for persistence."

"Can we fight them off?" asked William.

"The *Griffin* is a transport," said the Captain, "not a warship. She isn't heavily armed. Besides, that cruiser is four times our size."

"Can we outrun them then?" asked James.

"Most certainly," said the Captain, "if they don't send fighters after us."

"Sir," called Alex the radar tech, "several small contacts bearing on our position."

Captain Swift swore again,

"Now we don't have a choice," he said, "we're going to have to get rid of those fighters before they destroy our engines."

"Anything we can do?" asked Jon.

"Do you know how to work an AA gun?" asked the Captain.

"We can try," said Isaac.

"Good," said the Captain, "then get to your stations."

The travelers immediately scrambled from the bridge to help with the defense, but not all of them went to fight,

"Hey Matthias," said William.

"What?" asked Matthias.

"Would you help me with something?" asked William.

"Sure," said Matthias.

The two boys headed straight to the engine room to pitch an idea to Monty.

* * *

Though the *Griffin* was not heavily armed, its deck guns were nonetheless powerful. There were big twelve pound guns to protect against other ships and forty millimeter machine guns for anti-fighter defense. James, Krant, Jon, Loki and the Wolf brothers manned the machine guns alongside the crew. Jon pulled back the bolt of his gun with a ratcheting click,

"Lets rock and roll," he called to his friends. Isaac looked over at his brother,

"Is he always this eager for a fight?" he asked.

"Pretty much," said Scott, "I think it helps him get out his energy."

"Well," said Isaac, "we all need some way to vent

"Incoming!" shouted a crewman. Sure enough six fighter planes were heading towards them at high speed. They looked like a cross between an X-wing and a P-51 Mustang. The four-winged planes blazed over their heads, propeller blades buzzing loudly. The fighters banked around and came back on an attack run.

"Let 'em have it!" someone shouted. The *Griffin*'s gunners let loose a ratcheting volley of machine gun fire and two of the enemy planes streaked downward spewing smoke and flames.

"Ha ha," said Loki, "we got them."

"Not yet," called Jon, "there's still more."

Another fighter flew towards them, gun flashes blazing from the wings.

"Whoa," cried Loki as several rounds zipped past him, Scott let loose a short burst from his gun and severed two of the wings. The plane fell away from the *Griffin*, diving for the ocean at high speed.

"Three left!" cried a crewman.

The remaining planes streaked towards the *Griffin* and the gunners let off another volley of gunfire. Two of the fighters fell away trailing smoke, the last had its tail sliced off and tumbled into the sea below.

"That's it gents," came the Captain's voice over the intercom, "let's get out of here." There was a loud boom and a cloud of black smoke popped into being off the *Griffin*'s port quarter.

"The cruiser's shooting at us again," said the Captain, "get back inside. We'll try and out run them."

Everyone on the deck headed back into the ship for safety, the travelers headed for the bridge.

*   *   *

"Good work," Captain Swift told the travelers, "twelve planes in less than a minute. That's quite impressive."

"Thanks," said Isis, she and Katherine had downed four of them. The ship shuddered again.

"What are we going to do about that cruiser?" asked Mortimer.

"I believe I have the answer to that," said William as he entered the bridge.

"What do you mean?" asked the Captain.

"Would you mind handing me the intercom please Captain?" asked William.

Captain Swift handed the microphone to the book keeper.

"Engine room," said William.

"Go ahead laddie," responded Monty.

"I believe it's time to show the captain his new trick," said William.

"Aye," said Monty. William put the microphone back,

"You might want to hold on to something," he told everyone.

The subtle vibration from the engines suddenly increased to a rumble that nearly shook the teeth out of their mouths and the *Griffin* leaped forward with a boost of speed. The pursuing cruiser was left far behind as its prey shot off into a cloud bank.

CHAPTER FOUR:
A New Adventure

After escaping from Malagent's cruiser, the travelers were finally able to enjoy their cruise aboard the *Griffin*. Scott stood on the lounge balcony, leaning against the handrail as he watched the sunset. It was beautiful this high up, the rays of sun painting brilliant colors of red, orange, and purple across the clouds. He had untied his ponytail and let his long mane of hair billow in the wind. He heard the graceful footsteps of Isis coming up behind him; she wrapped her arms around him and leaned her head against his shoulder, he put his arm around her shoulders.

"It's been an interesting month hasn't it," He said.

"Yes," she said, "being transported to another world, meeting the twin brother you never knew you had. I'd certainly say it's been interesting."

"Yeah," said a voice, "all the cool stuff happened to you." It was Jon; he swaggered over and sat down on the rail.

"It's not like we wanted this to happen," said Isis.

"Yeah," said Jon, "I know."

"You know," said Scott, "they're not really all that different."

"What aren't?" asked Jon.

"The two worlds," said Scott, "Earth and Midaria."

"I guess so," agreed Jon, "blue skies, green grass. I could get used to living here." He yawned loudly, "Guess I'll head back to my room and get some shut eye."

Jon went inside the ship and headed for his stateroom. Scott and Isis stayed on the balcony watching the sunset before they went back to their room.

*   *   *

Sometime after night fall, Katherine found herself walking out on the balcony. She stood by the rail looking out into the night and wondered about what was going to happen to her and her friends. She felt a vague sense of things to come: good times and bad, hardship and adventure, joy and sadness. The night wind swirled these thoughts away as she shivered in the chill. She drew her cloak tighter around her for warmth and started heading back to her room when she heard a sound: a soft, hauntingly beautiful melody carried like dust on the wind. She walked towards the source of the sound to find Isaac Wolf sitting on the deck playing an ornately carved wooden flute. She stood watching as his fingers played over the instrument, masterfully shaping each note as it continued the song. He stopped when he noticed her,

"Lady Katherine," he said in his usual polite manner, "lovely evening wouldn't you say?"

"Yes," she said quietly.

"Are you troubled my lady?" asked Isaac.

"I'm worried about my friends," she told him, "I can't help feel that we'll never get home again."

"Home is wherever one chooses to make it," said Isaac, "But I think they'll be fine. After all, they have my brother to keep them safe."

"I know," said Katherine, "I still can't help but feel that way." She sat down next to him and leaned against the wall.

"Where did you learn to play?" she asked.

"I've always known," said Isaac with a slightly puzzled expression, "I can't really explain it."

"What were you playing?" asked Katherine, "it was beautiful."

"It was a lullaby," said Isaac, "I remember that my mother sang it to my brother and me."

"Can I hear it again?" asked Katherine.

"Certainly," said Isaac. He raised the flute to his lips and began playing again.

*   *   *

Matthias was having trouble sleeping. The bed in his room was soft enough, but the vibrations that resonated through the ship were too much for him to sleep soundly. He walked out into the corridor and headed downstairs to the galley for a glass of warm milk. He stopped suddenly halfway down the stairs. Drifting down from the lounge deck came the sound of someone playing a piano. It was a soft, steady melody that evoked feelings of travel. The young healer stood there for bit and listened to the music, it made him sleepy. Matthias' eyelids started feeling heavy as we walked back to his room.

He went back into his room and went straight to sleep. This time he slept quite soundly.

*   *   *

The next morning, Captain Swift joined his passengers for breakfast,

"We'll be arriving at Port Marraka tomorrow afternoon," he told them.

"What's like there?" asked William.

"Nice enough I suppose," said the Captain, "a bit crowded. But that's fairly typical of cities in Khartum."

"Khartum?" asked Katherine.

"It's the country we're heading to," said the Captain, "the whole place is a desert so most of the people live in cities."

"The Markets of Marraka are renowned as the busiest in the world," added Isaac.

"You've been there before I take it," said Mortimer.

"Once or twice," said Isaac.

"Good," said David, "you can help get supplies."

"What do you mean?" asked Jon.

"It's a desert," said Mortimer, "and unfortunately we're going to have to cross it."

"Couldn't we just fly the ship over it," said Jon.

"That desert is made of sun crystal," said the Captain, "airships can't fly over it."

"Great," said Mortimer sullenly, "a week long trek across the desert."

"What's with him?" Loki asked David.

"I'm from the country of Arkhan," said Mortimer, "it's very mountainous there."

"Morty doesn't like the heat," said David with a chuckle.

"There's only one thing you need to be warned about," said the Captain glancing at the thieves.

"What's that?" asked James.

"The penalty for stealing is having your hand cut off," said the Captain.

James gulped audibly and rubbed his wrists nervously.

*   *   *

The remainder of the cruise was uneventful and quite relaxing. The travelers spent the day playing cards in the lounge or enjoying the view from the balcony. Loki of course got along well the three thieves and managed to convince them to join in the fun. James and Krant turned out to be competent card players against William and Loki. Jessia helped the Wolf brothers convert the theatre into a training and sparring area. Isaac and Katherine spent quite a bit of time together and became very good friends, as did William and Matthias. Scott spent a lot of time in the library or hanging out with Isis. The *Griffin* made good time thanks to the improvements William had helped Monty with. Sure enough the ship arrived at Port Marraka exactly when Captain Swift said it would.

*   *   *

Port Marraka was a sprawling arabesque city with huge open air bazaars, towering minarets and lofty domes covered in brilliantly colored tiles. The harbor on the seaward side of the port was filled with ships of all sizes, from small fishing boats to huge cargo galleons, there were ships of both steam and sail. The landward side was dominated by the colossal aerodrome, the area for aircraft to land. There were other airships here, some even propelled by sails. There were heavier than air craft rather like the *Griffin* as well as blimps and zeppelins of various sizes. Numerous airplanes darted around and between the larger ships. After clearing their passage with the control tower, the *Griffin* came in to land. The ship swung around and descended into a landing gate, the four landing struts extending downward and settled on the ground with scarcely a bump. A footbridge extended out to connect with a staircase extending along the side of the ship from the lounge deck balcony. Captain Swift led his passengers across the bridge to where a tall, olive complexioned man in long robes was waiting for them. He bowed deeply as they approached,

"Salaam Alaaykum," he greeted them, "welcome to Port Marraka."

"Hello Zakeer," said the Captain some what surprised, "I thought the sultan's men had caught you and buried you out in the desert."

Zakeer laughed and smiled with straight but slightly yellowed teeth,

"Oh come now Gene," he said, "they know better than to get rid of their biggest supplier."

The travelers looked at the Captain quizzically,

"Zakeer is a merchant," said the Captain, "his wares are very cheap, but not always legal."

"I can't help it," said Zakeer, feigning innocence, "as a merchant it is my duty to find whatever my customer wants."

"Even black market sun crystals," the Captain said pointedly.

"You can pick them up off the ground here," said Zakeer, "why shouldn't anybody be able to sell them."

"Because it's illegal," said the Captain, "only the royal family can negotiate the sale of crystals."

"You're absolutely right," said Zakeer with a broad grin, "but even royalty have to get them from someone."

Both the merchant and the Captain burst out laughing.

"It's been too long my old friend," said Zakeer as he embraced the Captain.

"Yes it has," said the Captain.

"Come, "said Zakeer, "stay with me for dinner."

"Sure," said the Captain.

"Excellent," said Zakeer, "please, all of you follow me."

He led the travelers into the aerodrome complex.

"What was that about?" asked William.

"I used to be a naval officer," said the Captain, "fourteen years ago I would have been arresting him, but I left the military after the coup and his crystals power the *Griffin*, so I like to tease him every once in a while."

"You've gone soft Gene," said Mortimer.

"Watch it," warned the Captain.

Zakeer led them out of the aerodrome to three elegant looking motorcars waiting outside.

"You seem to be doing well Zakeer," said the Captain.

"What can I say," confessed Zakeer, "business has been good."

The travelers got into the cars and were driven away from the aerodrome and into the city. As they rode to Zakeer's home they looked out the windows at the people of the city. Merchants in street-side stalls haggled with their customers, bearded men sat in coffee and teahouses discussing local politics and business and occasionally smoking hookah pipes, women in colorful headscarves made their way around the shops buying household goods from the traders. The city was vibrant and colorful, beautiful woven carpets fluttered in the ocean breeze from balconies covered in colorful mosaic tiles, and tall, swaying palm trees and ferns added a lush, green look to this exotic port city.

*   *   *

Back at the aerodrome, the three thieves made their way off the *Griffin*,

"Come on," urged Krant, "it's completely safe."

"How can it be safe in a place where people cut your hands off if you steal anything," said James.

"That only happens if you get caught," Krant told him, "which we won't."

"Fine," said James, "but I still don't think this is a good idea."

"You'd rather stay on the ship," said Jessia, "you do know the crew are pirates."

"Pirates!" said James.

"Why do you think they had crates full of weapons," said Jessia.

"Okay," said James, "I'm going with you guys."

The thieves made their way through the aerodrome to the exit.

"What are we going to do now?" asked James, "Take a cab into town."

"Actually," said Krant, "we are."

Krant flagged down a taxi and the three rode into the city's market district. After paying the fare, James looked around for potential targets.

"Anything good?" asked Krant.

"I've got a few ideas," said James. He began outlining his plan.

*   *   *

Zakeer lived in a large, comfortable home on the seaward side of the city. The house was built from the same white mud brick as the rest of the city. Several balconies offered fantastic views of the city and the harbor; clearly it was the home of an extremely successful merchant.

"Welcome," said Zakeer, "please make yourselves comfortable."

The merchant's home was very tastefully decorated. Beautiful woven carpets covered the floors and curtains made of multi-colored wooden beads hung in doorways. A cool ocean breeze blew through the windows and gave the house a pleasant, homey air.

"Wow," said the Captain, "you have been doing well."

Zakeer just shrugged, "I do what I can," he said.

He introduced the travelers to his family: his wife Irana, his daughters Amina and Sari and his son Rajinn. Irana was a beautiful woman in sky blue robes and a white headscarf; her daughters were no less beautiful. Rajinn was a tall and skinny young man with his mother's darker complexion in a simple linen tunic and trousers. After the travelers introduced themselves, Zakeer showed them to the rooms he would be staying in. Isis and Katherine were given separate rooms on the opposite side of the house from the boys.

"This is pretty good," said Jon as he looked around the quarters he and the guys had been given, "these rooms are very comfortable."

After the travelers had settled into their accommodations Zakeer invited them to have dinner with his family. Everyone sat around a single, large table set with a platter of rice and vegetables. At each place setting was a small plate with a stack of pitas, to eat, one simply used the pitas to scoop what they wanted from the platter. There were bowls of various spices for flavor and brass pots of coffee and tea to drink.

"Wow," said Loki, "this is delicious."

"Thank you," said Irana, "it is the duty of all people to show warmth and hospitality to others."

"Very true," agreed Isaac, "would you please pass the curry?"

"Certainly," she passed him a bowl filled with a fine yellowish powder.

"So Zakeer," said Loki, "Captain Swift said you were a merchant. What do you sell?"

"Spices mostly," said Zakeer, "hence the mealtime fare."

"But you do sometimes sell things you're not supposed to right," said Matthias

"Most merchant's do that," said Zakeer, "its part of the job. I sell sun crystals to the sultan and his family, and they ensure that my regular business thrives by recommending my services to visiting dignitaries."

"Then I suppose you'd be able to get the supplies we need to cross the desert," said David.

"You're going to cross the desert on foot!" said Zakeer, "are you sure you want to do that?"

"It's only a little sand," said Jon, "How bad could it be?"

"Ever been in a sandstorm?" asked Mortimer. Jon shook his head.

"The wind blows the sand so hard it will peel flesh from bone. It's not pleasant."

"So what will you be needing?" asked Zakeer.

"I'll draw up a list," said David.

Dessert was served after dinner, delicious almond baklava smothered in honey. The sticky confection disappeared from the serving tray very quickly. After clearing the table and washing the dishes, Zakeer and his family went off to their evening prayers so the travelers decided to watch the sunset from the balconies. Isaac sat down on a wicker chair and looked out the sunlight sparkling across the water. Katherine joined him; she leaned against the rail with a worried look on her face.

"Are you troubled Lady Katherine?" he asked politely.

"No," said Katherine, "I'm just tired."

"Perhaps you should retire Lady Katherine," suggested Isaac.

"Why do you keep calling me that?" she asked, "I'm not nobility."

"It doesn't matter if you are nobility or not," said Isaac, "it is merely a term of respect."

"Oh," said Katherine, "Okay." She yawned deeply, "I guess I'll go to bed," she said.

"Goodnight Lady Katherine," said Isaac pleasantly. She went off to bed; he stayed on the balcony and watched the stars come out.

*   *   *

Tiramar, the capitol city of Veridea was once considered the most beautiful city in all of Midaria. All the buildings were constructed entirely of white marble. During the coup however, it had been severely damaged during the fighting that raged in the streets. The damage had never been repaired and this once vibrant and bustling city was now abandoned and silent as a tomb. It was to this city that Malagent had traveled to after the *Griffin* had escaped. He made his way through the empty, cratered streets to the royal palace. The once proud façade of the crown jewel of the once glorious city was now scarred and scorched by the artillery bombardment it had sustained during the battle.

After walking through the main gate he was met by the Royal Advisor, Verian Stormcrow. Verian was a large, broad-shouldered man with icy blue eyes and a demeanor to match. Malagent had never found any proof, but sometimes he would swear that if Verian looked at something long enough, it would freeze solid.

"Welcome home Malagent," said Verian, "I was beginning to think that doddering fool in Ikaros had discovered your plans and thrown you in his dungeon."

Malagent snorted derisively, "That 'sorcerer king' as he called himself wasn't worth the trouble. All that he did was read some old spell books and start having his subjects call him a sorcerer."

"Oh," said Verian, "so it was a waste of time like all the other missions you take upon yourself."

"Not entirely," retorted Malagent, "that's why I'm here."

"Well then," said Verian, "this way."

The Royal Advisor led the rodent-like man through the darkened hallways to the throne room. Verian paused before the door and fixed his gaze on Malagent. The little man instantly felt a chill, was that his breath he saw billowing from his mouth, he dismissed the thought as Verian began speaking,

"His majesty won't be pleased that you wasted valuable police time," he said, "Who knows, he might even have you replaced as Chief of the Dragon Eyes."

"I rather doubt that," said Malagent, after all if Alaraune got rid of him, his dream of a world without magically powered freaks would never come to fruition. Malagent stepped through the door to the throne room and began to approach the most powerful man in Veridea, perhaps even the world.

His Royal Majesty Alaraune Draconan, the All-watching King of Veridea sat in his carved wooden throne with his head tilted backwards and his eyes shut.

"Ah Malagent," said Alaraune, "I've been expecting you." His voice had the rich timbre and calm tone of a charismatic leader.

"Your Majesty," began Malagent, "I have come to report that--"

"I know," interrupted Alaraune, "the 'sorcerer king' of Ikaros was a fraud."

"Yes," said Malagent nervously, he should have expected that.

"But that is not all you have to say is it not?" asked Alaraune.

"No my lord," said Malagent, "it is not. There was something else, a book that the false sorcerer had recovered from a young thief that came to his castle."

Alaraune leaned his head forward and opened his left eye, the one not obscured by his long, grayed hair.

"Tell me off this book," he said, "describe it."

"It was faced with blue leather and etched with runes of great power," said Malagent, "the book was stolen by another group of young people; it was they who killed the king of Ikaros."

Alaraune seemed interested, he leaned forward and listened intently,

"Tell me more about this book," he said, "why was the king so interested in it."

"He claimed it was a source of ultimate power," said Malagent, "it was just delusional nonsense."

Alaraune's eye widened, "He's found it!" he exclaimed. The King of Veridea stood up from his throne and began to walk from the room, Malagent followed him.

"Found what my lord?" he asked.

"The Book of Power," said Alaraune.

"It couldn't be," said Malagent, "the book was lost after the coup."

"Not entirely," said Alaraune, "the Book of Power was sent away to another world, but it belongs to this one. No matter how far it is sent away it will eventually return, and now it has."

Alaraune opened the side door of the throne room and the two men walked out into the hallway.

"Malagent," said Alaraune, "I want you to find this book."

"I have my lord," said Malagent, "it is in the possession of the young people who killed the king. And it was them I was going to tell you of next."

"What about them?" asked Alaraune.

"Two of them bear the mark of the sorcerers," said Malagent, "one is a young woman with black hair and green eyes, the other is a tall young man with grey eyes. The young man seems familiar somehow."

"Really," said Alaraune.

"Yes," said Malagent, "he has a twin brother, if not for the white hair of the one, it would be almost impossible to tell them apart."

"So it's true then," said Alaraune.

"What's true my lord?" asked Malagent.

"Those twin brothers you saw," said Alaraune, "were the Wolf brothers."

"Impossible!" said Malagent in disbelief, "how do you know this?"

Alaraune took the lock of hair and tucked it behind his ear, Malagent hated this part.

"I have seen them," said Alaraune. He opened his other eye, while his majesty's left eye was the same green one he was born with his right was something completely different. It was dark red streaked gold with a diamond shaped pupil, Alaraune Draconan's right eye was the all-seeing eye of a dragon.

Malagent gulped nervously,

"What do you wish of me my lord?" he asked.

"Bring me these young people and the book, I wish to meet the Wolf brothers and finish what I began fourteen years ago."

"Yes my lord," said Malagent, "I'll send my finest Dragon Eyes to Port Marraka at once."

"No," said Alaraune, "by the time your men arrive they would be too late. Send your men to Dalamasc, have them set up a 'welcoming party' for these young people."

"Yes my lord," said Malagent, "at once."

He bowed to his king and headed off to fulfill his masters wishes.

End of Book One